Fast and Dangerous Times

Joe hit the pedals of his bike and lurched out of the starting gate and down the steep, bare ski slope.

"Yahoo!" he whooped. Yelling wasn't very professional, but the thrill of descent felt glorious. Stones and dust kicked up behind Joe as he zoomed toward the first turn.

He came in hard and clenched the hand brake to slow himself a little. The bike skidded sideways a bit, costing him some time, but he regained control and headed for the second steep turn.

A tall stand of pines rose up before him as he neared a jog to the right. He squeezed the brakes lightly to take the edge off the turn.

The grips caught for a moment, then pressed all the way to the handlebars. The brakes didn't catch. Unable to control his speed, Joe careened toward the tall pine trees.

The Hardy Boys Mystery Stories

Available from MINSTREL Books and ALADDIN Paperbacks

THE **HARDY BOYS**®

#173

SPEED TIMES FIVE

FRANKLIN W. DIXON

Aladdin Paperbacks
New York London Toronto Sydney Singapore

First Aladdin Paperbacks edition June 2002

Copyright © 2002 by Simon & Schuster, Inc.

ALADDIN PAPERBACKS
An imprint of Simon & Schuster
Children's Publishing Division
1230 Avenue of the Americas
New York, NY 10020

The text of this book was set in New Caledonia.

Printed in the United States of America
2 4 6 8 10 9 7 5 3 1

THE HARDY BOYS and THE HARDY BOYS MYSTERY
STORIES are trademarks of Simon & Schuster, Inc.

Library of Congress Control Number: 2001098777

ISBN 0-7434-3746-2

Contents

1 To the Mountaintop

"Pull ahead and get out of the car," said the Canadian border guard.

Joe Hardy pulled the van into the indicated parking space, and he, his brother, Frank, Chet Morton, and Jamal Hawkins got out.

"Is there any trouble, Officer Benson?" Joe asked, reading the nametag on the guard's lapel.

Officer Benson, a balding, middle-aged man with a short beard shook his head. He and a female guard opened the van's doors and looked inside. They peered under the seats, into the back, in the glove compartment, and into the spare tire well. "Just a routine check," Benson said.

"I never thought there'd be much call for smuggling from America to Canada, or vice versa," Jamal said good-naturedly.

"You'd be surprised," Officer Benson replied.

"Cigarettes, alcohol, medicine, weapons," the woman officer, whose name badge read Scott, replied. She finished peering at the van's underside and added, "Even exotic animals."

"Any of those clinging to the van's underside?" Chet asked with a grin.

Officer Scott smiled back. "Not a one."

"I need to check your IDs," Officer Benson said. He looked over the four friends' birth certificates and asked, "What's the purpose of your visit to Canada and how long will you be staying?"

"We're here to compete in the Speed Times Five race at the Fire Creek Mountain Resort," Frank said.

"That's what all the gear in back is for," Joe added. Officer Scott carefully checked through their equipment as the teens spoke to Officer Benson. "We'll be in the country about a week," the younger Hardy finished.

Benson nodded. "Can I see your race entry forms, please?"

"Sure thing," Frank said, digging their registration forms out of his luggage. "Joe and I are competing; Chet and Jamal are our support team."

"All this seems to be in order," Benson said. "Did you find anything, Officer Scott?"

"Nothing unusual," Officer Scott replied. She turned to the four friends and asked, "Is this the cross-border race from the Laurentians to Vermont?"

"That's the one," Joe said.

"Biking, hiking, climbing, and a water race," Jamal added. "It's a real test of skill and endurance."

"Well, good luck," Officer Benson said, handing back their papers. "You can go."

The four friends piled into the van and soon left the border crossing behind. They headed north, leaving the wooded back roads near the U.S.–Canadian border and joining Highway 133 heading for Montreal.

As they drove, Chet fiddled with the radio, changing from one station to the next.

"What are you looking for, Chet?" Joe, behind the wheel once more, asked.

"I was hoping to hear something about the race," Chet replied, "but I can't find anything in English."

"I learned some French to help my dad out," Jamal offered. Jamal's father ran an air taxi service and sometimes had dealings with the Canadian cities of Montreal and Quebec. "Let me give it a try." He scanned the dial for a few minutes, listening intently.

"Anything interesting?" Frank asked.

"Stuff about the prime minister and a trade deal, a break-in at a pharmaceutical plant, some news about a local Native American protest group . . . Oh, wait. Here's something. It's a promo ad for the race, celebrating the reopening of the Fire Creek Mountain Resort."

"Well," Chet said, "I guess that qualifies, but I was hoping for something a bit more."

"That's our Chet," Joe said jokingly, "always looking for publicity. You'd think he'd be satisfied after his brief stint as a TV star." Joe spotted the exit they needed and took it north, past Montreal and into the Laurentian Mountains.

"Don't worry, Chet," Frank added. "The race crews never get the glory anyway."

Chet shrugged. "I'm not asking for national coverage," he said. "I just thought the race would get more notice."

"There are plenty of reality shows on the box already," Jamal said. "Now, if you added some stock cars . . ."

They wound their way through the scenic roads between Montreal and the mountains north of the city. As they left the suburbs behind, summer forests sprang up around them, leading in a continuous green swath up toward the Laurentians.

They passed the town of St. Esprit and turned off the highway shortly thereafter. Frank checked the map while Joe drove, keeping them on course through the wooded back roads.

"This sure is a strange time to head for a ski resort," Jamal observed.

"The resort is only the starting point for the competition," Joe said. "They're using the downhill ski slopes for the first leg of the mountain bike race."

"The race will follow the same track we're taking to reach the resort, right?" Chet asked.

"More or less," Frank replied.

"Of course, during the race we'll be traveling

through the countryside," Joe added. "I don't think we see any real roads until the fifth day or so."

"You know," Jamal said, "there have been times when I wished I'd entered this race myself." A broad smile broke across his handsome brown face. "Then I think of all the dirt and the bugs and the poison ivy and the lack of food and water . . . and then I'm glad to be on your support team instead." He laughed and the others laughed with him.

By the middle of the afternoon, the Hardys, Chet, and Jamal reached the Fire Creek Mountain Resort. After checking their passes, a guard waved them through to the parking lot reserved for competitors.

"Boy! Look at all the sponsor stickers on those cars!" Chet said. Colorful decals with the names of sodas, sports equipment, medical technology suppliers, and Web sites decorated many of the vans and SUVs parked in the lot. There were also a number of trucks decked out with television broadcast dishes.

"These mostly look like local stations," Jamal said, checking out the TV call letters, "though there's one from the UAN network, as well."

"That makes sense," Joe said. "UAN is planning to cut the race footage together into a show for broadcast later. We had to sign a TV release when we registered."

"I'm seeing stickers from some pretty big sponsors," Chet said. "I saw a TV show on LaTelle Medical and Pharmaceutical. Their founder, Phil LaTelle, built them up from nothing, and now they're at the cutting edge of medicine and technology. SeaZoom, QuickAid, and StarTel are big companies, too."

"I guess your worries about lack of publicity were unfounded, Chet," Frank said. He and the others got out of the van and walked across the parking lot toward a small collection of buildings at the base of the ski slopes.

The Fire Creek Mountain lodges had the look of an old-time resort. The buildings' walls were made from cut logs, and wooden shingles adorned their roofs. A large, central hotel dominated the other buildings. It was three stories tall and had large banks of windows overlooking the natural beauty that surrounded it.

The resort's scenery was breathtaking. Pristine mixed-wood forests reached up the mountainside like blue-green fingers. A mixture of new green grass, moss, and tan earth covered the ski runs. In the distance, the Laurentian Mountains stretched toward the deep blue sky.

Numerous ski-lift cable lines traced up the mountainside, winding between the trees and the ski trails. Sleek, modern lift platforms stood at the bottom of the slopes.

A sign reading Competitor Sign-In directed the teens toward a smaller building with a high-peaked roof. Joe and Frank noted that despite the resort's old-fashioned appearance, none of the wood on the buildings' exteriors looked very weathered. They had all either been recently constructed or recently restored.

"Nice place," Jamal noted as they walked toward the smaller building.

"Yeah," Chet said. "Winning a year-long pass to this place would be pretty cool." He winked at Jamal. "Let's hope our racers come through for us and win that prize!"

"We'll do okay," Joe replied, "assuming our support team can cut it." He grinned.

"A prize would be nice," Frank said, "but we're in this for the competition."

Chet rolled his eyes. "Not the prizes, not the glory . . ."

"And with Callie and Iola at home," Jamal added, "definitely not the girls." He reached for the door handle of the registration building and was nearly bowled over as the door flew open and a man burst out.

"Oh! Sorry, mates!" the man said. He was slightly shorter than the teens but solidly built. He wore a floppy beige hat, matching fatigues, and an equipment vest. With his clothes and his five o'clock shadow, he looked like an escapee from a jungle adventure movie. He smiled at the four friends.

"You're competitors, right?" he said. "I can always spot 'em. I'm Vince Bennett, the race organizer." He extended his hand and shook with all four of them.

"I'm Jamal Hawkins," Jamal said. "The big guy is Chet Morton, the blond is Joe Hardy, and the dark-haired one is his brother, Frank."

"Pleased to meet you," Joe, Frank, and Chet said.

"Pleased to meet you all, too," Bennett said, flashing a set of perfect teeth. "Get yourselves checked in. I've got some last-minute fires to put out, but I'm giving all the racers a rundown on the event later."

"We're looking forward to it," Frank said.

"Great," Bennett said. He turned and sprinted off toward the main lodge.

"He seems just the same as he does on TV," Chet said.

"Yeah," Jamal said. "I've caught a couple of his previous adventure races."

"Somehow," Frank said, "I doubt this will be as perilous as swimming with sharks in Australia."

"Or hiking across an active volcano in Chile," Joe added.

Jamal held the door and all four of them went inside. "Still," he said, "there's always some kind of danger in a Bennett-sponsored race."

"I don't know if I'd call it *danger*," Chet replied, "more like . . . *excitement*."

It took the Hardys and their crew a half hour to check in and get all their paperwork cleared. Other competitors drifted in and out of the registration lodge as the teens worked. Some competitors had complaints; others were completing their paperwork like the Hardys. As the friends finished the last of their forms, a tall, thin, bearded man wearing a red T-shirt and jeans stalked in.

"Well," he said angrily, "it looks like I'll have to sign up for a race-sponsored support team after all. My trainer got into a car accident on his way through Wisconsin. He's laid up with a busted leg and can't make it for the race."

The woman working the registration desk looked perplexed. "Mr. Lupin, I'm not sure that we have any support teams still available."

"That's Michael Lupin," Chet whispered to the others. "He was on one of those TV survival shows."

"Did he survive?" Jamal whispered with a smile.

Chet shook his head. "No. He was voted off."

"Julie, I know it's inconvenient," Michael Lupin said, speaking to the registration woman, "but we both know that I'm one of the reasons people might tune in to see this show. Ask Bennett if he wants me sitting out the race."

Julie frowned. "I'll see what I can do," she said.

Lupin nodded. "Good. Thanks. I knew you'd come through for me. I'm taking the lift up to the summit lodge. I'll take the good news there." He turned and left the building.

Joe and Frank handed in the last of their paperwork. "Tough customer, that guy," Joe said to Julie, the registration woman.

Julie shrugged. "No tougher than most of the competitors. Though I'm sure he wants you to think so." She smiled and handed the teens their race ID tags. "There are two lifts to the big summit lodge," she said. "The gondola will take your bikes up. You can either go up with them, or you can take the high-speed quad. It's open-air, so you get a better view, and it's faster as well."

"Chet and I will take the bikes and equipment up if you want to ride the quad," Jamal said.

"Sounds good," Frank replied. "We'll help you load the stuff first, though."

The four of them unloaded their gear from the van and took it to the gondola platform. Then Frank and Joe headed for the quad chairlift.

When the brothers arrived, there were two other people waiting for the next chair. One was Michael Lupin. The other was a short, tanned woman with long, straight black hair. She wore a black muscle shirt, and jeans with an ornate beaded belt. She and Lupin stood silently, watching the lift approach. A race staff member checked Joe's and Frank's credentials as they passed.

"Hi," Joe said as the brothers approached Lupin and the woman. "Joe and Frank Hardy."

"Michael Lupin," Lupin said, shaking hands.

"Kelly Hawk," the woman said, doing the same. "Are you boys racers, or support?"

"Racers," Frank replied.

Lupin and Hawk nodded.

The chairlift arrived, and the four of them seated themselves. In a few moments they were whizzing up the mountainside, suspended from a cable high in the air.

Frank and Joe watched the scenery as they rode. The view was spectacular, taking in Fire Creek

Mountain, the resort below, and the wooded countryside and mountains beyond. The late afternoon sun painted the trees and hillsides a golden color. Ahead lay the summit lodge, a hotel-like structure whose high roofs and many windows echoed the larger buildings of the resort below.

As they drew within thirty yards of the top, the chairlift jerked and bounced on the cable. The chair came to a sudden stop and swayed precariously in the wind.

Joe and Frank looked down. "If this chair lets go," Frank said to his brother, "we'll need a parachute to survive."

2 A Long Way Down

Kelly Hawk looked around nervously as a vibration from the cable made the chairlift shudder. "What do you think happened?" she asked.

"Some kind of mechanical problem, I'd guess," Frank said.

"I'm sure they'll have it sorted out in a couple of minutes," Joe added.

Michael Lupin checked his watch. "They'd better," he said. "No way I'm spending the rest of the afternoon in this chairlift."

The lift swayed dangerously on the cable. "Just stay calm," Frank said. "They'll fix it soon."

Ahead of them, the next loaded chair had already made it to the platform. Downhill, another set of passengers dangled nervously in the air.

Joe gazed up at the hardware securing the lift to

the steel cable. All the connections looked intact. "Frank's right," Joe said. "We're not in any danger here. We should just sit tight."

Kelly Hawk, seated on the far end of the chair, looked skeptically at the two of them. "You guys are brothers, right? Do you always agree on everything?"

The Hardys chuckled. "Not nearly," Frank said.

"But we've been in a few tight scrapes before," Joe added, "and come out okay."

"Forgive me for not being more trusting," Hawk said, "but my people have gotten some bad advice over the years."

"Your people? What do you mean?" Joe asked.

"I belong to the Fire Creek Mohawks," Hawk said. "My ancestors roamed the land from the Laurentians to New Hampshire's White Mountains long before Europeans came to this continent. This land used to be ours."

"And you want it back, I suppose," Lupin said, somewhat annoyed.

Hawk scowled at him. "Some of it, yes. We'd like to keep some of the streams clear of industrial pollution and some of the mountainsides free from clear-cutting."

"So you're entering the race to publicize your cause?" Frank asked.

Kelly Hawk nodded. "Among other reasons."

"While we were driving here, we heard something on the radio about Native American protests," Joe said.

13

"That's our lawyers fighting it out in court," Hawk said. "I don't go for that stuff. I'm a one-woman protest and publicity campaign."

"Well, good luck," Frank said.

"Both in the race and with your political efforts," Joe added.

"Thanks," Hawk said with a wry smile. "Maybe you two aren't as boring and straightlaced as you seem."

"Before this becomes a mutual admiration society," Lupin said, "you should know I'm not here to make friends; I'm in this race to *win.*"

"And to make up for your loss on *Last Person Standing*?" Hawk asked.

"I nearly won on the show," Lupin countered. "And I'm going to win here." He checked his watch again.

"I crossed a rope bridge hand-over-hand in Borneo," Lupin said. "This cable is a lot sturdier than that. You can wait if you want to, but if this chair gives way, I'm not going to be sitting here when it happens." He began to raise the safety bar.

"Don't be an idiot," Hawk said. "That was a TV show, this is real life."

"Hey, the *danger* was real," Lupin shot back.

Frank grabbed Lupin's shoulder. "Don't do it," he said. "Standing up in this chair could endanger us all."

"We're in this together," Hawk said, "so sit down and wait patiently with the rest of us."

Lupin glanced from Frank to Joe to Hawk. He

14

lowered the safety bar. "Yeah, okay," he said. "I won't wait forever, though."

"Tough break your trainer landing in the hospital," Frank said.

Lupin nodded grimly. "I'm not too happy about using a race-sponsored support crew," he said.

"I thought all competitors brought their own support people," Joe said.

"Not everyone has their own team," Hawk replied. "The race hires crews for racers who don't bring their own."

"For a fee," Lupin added. He crossed his arms over his chest and grumbled, "Makes me feel like an amateur."

Just then the chairlift gave a jerk and started moving again.

Moments later they all landed on the staging platform near the summit lodge. A young man wearing a badge that said, Staff: Kendall, quickly walked over to the group. "I am *so* sorry," he said.

"What happened?" Frank asked.

"Something got jammed in the chairlift equipment at the bottom of the slope," Kendall replied. "Fortunately, no one was hurt. Mr. Lupin, we've found a new support team for you. If you'd follow me, please . . . The rest of you can hook up with your crews and equipment at the summit lodge."

"Good deal," Joe said. He, Frank, and Kelly Hawk headed for the main lodge while Lupin followed Kendall toward an A-frame building marked Administration.

As the Hardys and Hawk neared the lodge entrance, a man and a woman in matching red-and-white uniforms came out of the main doors.

"Ms. Hawk," the woman said, a look of disapproval marring her pretty face, "my brother and I think it is wrong of you to use this race for your political purposes."

"As opposed to the commercial purposes you and your brother are using it for, Victoria?" Hawk said archly.

"We have entered the race for the thrill of the competition," the man said. "If our fame is spread by our victories"—he shrugged—"so much the better."

"Georges," Hawk said, "you'd give your eye teeth to get an American sponsor endorsement—don't pretend you wouldn't."

"No need to be hostile about this," Victoria said. "Perhaps we could have a more civilized discussion some other time."

Hawk's dark brown eyes narrowed. "Are you calling me a savage?" she hissed.

The man and woman looked shocked. "No, no," Georges said. "We did not intend it that way. Just, perhaps, that we should speak later. Adieu." He and his sister turned and jogged off together toward the administration building.

"Who were they?" Joe asked.

"Victoria and Georges Clemenceau," Hawk said. "Hotshot local athletes looking to make their names across the border. Snobs." She turned her head and spat onto the grass. "Look, I'll see you boys later. I've got some things to do." She turned and headed toward the gondola platform, pulling a cell phone out of her pocket as she went.

"Why didn't she use the phone when we were trapped on the chairlift?" Joe asked, slightly annoyed.

Frank shrugged. "I guess she wasn't any more worried than we were," he said. He pushed open the door to the main lodge and they both went inside.

The entry opened into a large, wide room with a high ceiling supported by huge timber beams. On one side, a lounge with tall floor-to-ceiling windows looked out over the ski slopes. A large stone fireplace was set in a short wall between the windows. Tables and chairs surrounded the fireplace, which—due to the season—had no fire burning in it.

To the right of the entryway, a passage led from the main room to the guest rooms beyond. To the left sat the lodge's registration desk, which was serving as a check-in area for the contestants.

Joe and Frank went to the desk and checked themselves in. The clerk behind the counter assigned them a room for the night and gave them a set of keys.

"The last real bed we'll see for a while," Joe said, wagging the keys in his hand. "Enjoy it while you can."

Frank was about to reply when the door of the lodge burst open and a tall, burly man surged through. "Outrageous!" he said, almost shouting.

17

"Someone could have been hurt. Why wasn't the lift checked before the event started?"

A member of the race staff trailed after him, nodding obsequiously. "I assure you, Mr. Baldwin, the lifts *were* checked before anyone used them. It was an accident, that's all."

Behind Baldwin and the staff member came three college students—two men and a woman— all wearing UMass T-shirts.

"Well, tell Bennett that he needs to get his act together," Baldwin said. He stalked over to the desk and held out his hand. "Give me my room key."

"Who's that?" Joe whispered as he and Frank walked away from the desk.

"Roger Baldwin," offered one of the students, a thin man with dark curly hair and big sideburns. "He's a former Ironman triathlete, and I guess he's trying to switch sports." The student extended his hand. "I'm Quentin Curtis. These are my friends, Maggie Collins and Robert Frid." The other two, a man with short black hair and a woman with long auburn tresses, offered their hands as well.

The Hardys shook hands with them. "Frank and Joe Hardy," Frank said.

"Are you three a team?" Joe asked.

"No," Frid said. "We're all competing separately."

"Though not in a cutthroat way," Maggie Collins added with a smile. "What about you two?"

"We're competing as well," Frank said. "Our support crew should be here shortly."

"When Frank says 'crew' he actually means our friends Chet Morton and Jamal Hawkins," Joe said, grinning.

"We're using hired support," Curtis said. "One of the college alumni pitched in on the cost so all of us could race."

"Lucky thing," Frid added, "or two of us would just be along for the ride."

"Well, nice meeting you," Frank said. "I'm sure we'll see more of each other during the race bivouacs. C'mon, Joe. We'd better find Jamal and Chet."

The Hardys left the hilltop lodge and joined up with their friends at the gondola platform. They checked over their mountain bikes, and housed them in a large shed being used to store race equipment. Then all four scouted the next day's downhill course before returning to the lodge for dinner. After dinner, they mingled and scoped out their rivals some more.

The large field of competitors came from all over the northeastern United States and Canada. Most had joined up for the thrill of the race. Many were college students like Curtis, Frid, and Collins. Others, like Roger Baldwin, had crossed over from other athletic disciplines. Some, like the Clemenceaus, hoped to expand their media visibility. A few, like Hawk and Lupin, seemed driven by their own inner fires.

Most of the contestants kept to themselves during the evening and retired early, not wanting to betray their strategies to their rivals. The Hardys, Jamal, and Chet turned in just before ten.

Morning dawned bright and beautiful over Fire Creek Mountain. Sunlight blazed over the green ridges of the resort and painted the bare ski slopes orange and gold.

The Hardys and their friends rolled out of the sack early and joined the other competitors in the dining hall for breakfast. Then the brothers went to the equipment shed and gave their mountain bikes a last going-over.

As the starting time drew near, the race crew assembled the contestants in front of the lodge, and Vince Bennett spoke to the group.

"Greetings! Welcome to the Speed Times Five Adventure Race!" Bennett called to the crowd through a bullhorn. "Glad to see you all up and at 'em this early." He smiled as the competitors grumbled back a sleepy greeting. "Hopefully, all of you received your start times with your competitor's package when you checked in. For the benefit of the media present"—he nodded to a stand of video cameras set up nearby—"let me explain that the racers will start in order of ranking—for those who have competed in previous adventure races—or by random group draw for new participants."

"How'd we do on start time?" Chet asked.

"Not too bad," Frank said, checking his schedule.

"We're about the middle of the pack. I'm going before Joe."

"They kept us together since we're using the same support crew," Joe said, smiling at Chet and Jamal.

"Because of the staggered start, the racers will be timed to the checkpoints," Bennett continued. "These times will determine starting order during other legs of the race. The media and spectators can check the Speed Times Five Web site for complete rules.

"Racers' communications packs will be given a once-over by race personnel at every checkpoint. Because of the isolation of parts of the course, it is *vital* that you keep your communications gear in good working condition.

"Also, please observe the rules of good sportsmanship. If someone is in trouble, make sure you help him or her or—at the very least—call for assistance. The race can be dangerous; let's look out for one another.

"Finally, I want to thank our support staff and race sponsors, especially StarTel communications, QuickAid sports drinks, the Tuffy bike corporation, LaTelle Medical and Pharmaceutical, and Sea-Zoom personal water craft. And, of course, I can't forget the beautiful Fire Creek Mountain Resort, who have allowed us the use of their spectacular facilities for the first three stages of this race. Next time you're in Quebec, visit Fire Creek Mountain."

Bennett gazed out over the sea of eager racers assembled before him. "So, are you ready to race?"

"Yeah!" the crowd screamed back.

"Then let's hit the starting blocks!" Bennett waved to the crowd, pointed toward the starting gate atop the ski hill, and then jogged in that direction.

Half an hour later, the Hardys' starting numbers were called, and the team made its way to the gate.

"See you both at the first resupply point," Jamal said.

"Take good care of the van," Frank said.

"We'll treat it as if we owned it," Chet replied.

"That's what we're worried about," Joe shot back jokingly.

A crowd of officials milled around the starting gate. They checked the communications equipment—a durable long-range walkie-talkie hooked into race headquarters—as each racer came through, and ran through a final prerace checklist.

Joe and Frank completed their paperwork and headed for the gate. Ahead of them, the brothers saw Kelly Hawk plunge down the slope at a breakneck pace. Collins, Frid, and Curtis waited nearby, looking very much a team in their matching UMass campus wear. All of the students started before Joe and Frank.

When his turn came, Frank mounted his bike at the top of the run. He gave Joe the thumbs-up, waited for the starting buzzer, and then took off downhill.

Joe positioned his mountain bike in the starting gate and hopped on. He watched as Frank zipped around the first turn in the course, disappearing behind a stand of pine trees. Joe looked at the starter, who said, "Ready?"

Joe nodded and adjusted his racing helmet and goggles. The starter brought up his starting timer, which was hooked into the gate. The lights on either side of the gate flashed red . . . yellow . . . green! A buzzer sounded and the gate flew open.

Joe hit the pedals and lurched out of the gate and down the steep, bare ski slope.

"Yahoo!" he whooped. Yelling wasn't very professional, but the thrill of descent felt glorious. Stones and dust kicked up behind Joe as he zoomed toward the first turn.

He came in hard and clenched the hand brake to slow himself a little. The bike skidded sideways a bit, costing him some time, but he regained control and headed for the second steep turn.

A tall stand of pines rose up before him as he neared a jog to the right. He squeezed the brakes lightly to take the edge off the turn.

The grips caught for a moment, then pressed all the way to the handlebars. The brakes didn't catch. Unable to control his speed, Joe careened toward the tall pine trees.

3 Accidental Meetings

Joe squeezed the brakes once more as he turned the bike's front wheel to steer away from the edge of the course.

Nothing. He had no brakes at all.

He flipped the shift lever and kicked the bike into a lower gear, hoping he wouldn't throw the chain as he did so. The chain held and the bike turned, but not fast enough.

Trees shot up in front of him, a dense, green wall. Many of the trunks were a foot wide. The mesh ski fencing at the edge of the course looked flimsy and inadequate. Joe doubted it would stop him from a nasty spill.

Desperate, he leaned the bike sideways while he continued to try to turn. If he tipped too far, the controlled slide he was aiming for would turn into a bruising skid. The bike's wide tires bit into the rough dirt, spraying pebbles and dust into the air.

Nearly digging the bike's right pedal into the dirt, Joe veered away from the ski fence and the tall trees. He tried to turn the bike back uphill, to use the lower gear as a breaking mechanism, but his momentum was too great. He'd avoided an initial crash but kept hurtling down the hill at frightening speed.

He and the bike went airborne as the ground dipped on the next straightaway. Joe held his breath and braced for the landing, concentrating on maintaining control of the bike. The impact made his bones ache, but he held on tight and the bike stayed under him.

As he landed, Joe caught sight of Frank ahead of him, gliding into the next big turn. Joe snaked back and forth across the course, trying to slow his descent. When he reached the turn, though, he had to abandon that strategy or risk a bad spill.

The course turned to the left now and cut back quickly several times from right to left and back. Joe careened from one side of the course to the other, trying to burn up some of the bike's momentum. He swung perilously close to ski fences and obstacles on both sides as he went.

Once, his tires skidded out from under him and he had to touch his foot down to keep from falling. A sharp pain shot up from his ankle to his knee. Joe gritted his teeth and held on for dear life.

He went airborne again near the bottom of the hill and was surprised to spot Frank right in front of him. The elder Hardy had steered a far more conservative course and looked in full control of his bike.

Joe swerved to avoid hitting Frank and could only imagine the look on his older brother's face as he shot past. A checkpoint loomed at the bottom of the hill as the slope flattened out, but Joe couldn't stop. Collins, Frid, and Curtis stood waiting to be cleared through the checkpoint as Joe plummeted toward them.

The course turned ninety degrees to the left at the checkpoint. Joe knew he'd never make the turn. He zipped past the startled college students and plummeted into the forest. The calls of the race officials echoed after him for a moment before being drowned out by the sound of his mountain bike crashing through the light underbrush.

The younger Hardy wove his crippled bike between the trees, barely missing the wide trunks. Fortunately, the rough terrain and brush beneath the pines soon diminished the bike's speed. Joe put his feet down and slid to a stop just short of a huge spruce. He whistled a long, slow sigh of relief.

Joe got off the bike and looked back to see Frank sprinting through the forest toward him. "Joe!" the older Hardy called. "Are you all right?"

"Fine," Joe called back. "Just a bit shook up."

Frank skidded to a halt next to his brother. "What's wrong?" the older Hardy asked. "Why didn't you stop at the checkpoint?"

"I couldn't," Joe said. "Something's wrong with my brakes." He knelt down by the front wheel; Frank did the same at the back.

Frank frowned. "The cable's come loose from the brake mechanism," he said.

"Up here, too," Joe said. "I know we checked the connections last night. They were working fine when I took the bike out of the shed this morning, too."

"It wouldn't take someone too long to loosen the nuts holding the cables," Frank said.

"But the bike's been with me the whole time," Joe said.

"Not when we did the final paperwork and communications check," Frank said. "We racked the bikes then."

"But who would want to sabotage my bike?" Joe asked. "It doesn't make sense."

Frank nodded. "You're right. It's not like we're big-name competitors or anything." He shrugged. "Maybe it's just a bad break—no pun intended. C'mon. Let's get your bike fixed so we can get back into the race."

The brothers walked back through the woods toward the checkpoint. As they went, several out-of-breath race staffers ran up to them. "Are you all right?" one asked.

"I had a problem with the brakes," Joe said. "But I should be able to fix it and continue."

"You really had us worried," said the other official. "Vince Bennett saw the video feed and called

27

to check on you. We're glad you're okay." As he talked, the other official radioed in the news that Joe hadn't been hurt.

The four of them returned to the checkpoint in time to see Roger Baldwin pedaling off down the cross-country trail. Michael Lupin arrived at the bottom of the hill as the brothers unpacked their emergency repair kits and began working on Joe's bike. Lupin spared the brothers only a glance before finishing his check-in and biking down the trail.

It took the Hardys only a few minutes to make the needed repairs. They tested Joe's brakes vigorously, then completed the checkpoint routine and headed into the forest. The cross-country trail was more suited to hiking or skiing than bike racing. Pine needles made traction difficult and the course wound up and downhill frequently.

Joe soon began to feel the effects of his ordeal. His muscles ached and his breath came in labored gasps. "Go ahead of me, Frank," he said. "You can make better time than I can."

"No way," Frank replied. "I don't care if we've both got emergency radios. I'd rather stick close and rely on each other."

A few racers passed the brothers as they rode in tandem through the forested hills. The Hardys passed several competitors as well. Some were merely going slow, others had troubles of their own. One woman had a broken bicycle frame and was using her radio to call for help. Another man was sitting by the side of the trail, taking an early break to drink some water.

"Bet that guy doesn't finish in the top ten," Joe said with a tired grin.

Several helicopters passed overhead as they labored up and down the terrain.

"Media?" Joe asked.

"Or race monitors or medical personnel," Frank suggested. "I thought I spotted the Red Cross and the LaTelle Medical logo on a chopper earlier. Either way, I'm glad someone's keeping an eye on things."

"The choppers kind of spoil the pristine atmosphere, though," Joe said.

Frank chuckled. "Like a bunch of people on mountain bikes don't?"

They stopped only briefly for a packed lunch, to stretch, and to recheck the gear on the bikes.

"This course is jostling things all out of whack," Joe said, tugging his handlebars back into proper alignment.

"It could have been your earlier run off the mountain, too," Frank replied.

"Not the best start," Joe said, "but we're making up some ground—even if my whole body aches."

"Just wait until day six," Frank said.

Joe smiled. "You'll be eating my dust by then, bro."

"We'll see about that," Frank replied. He mounted up and rode off. Joe did the same, only a second or two behind.

The beauty of the woodland scenery took some of the monotony out of the rolling hills. Soon the pines of the mountain slope gave way to a mixed forest: maples, oaks, and other deciduous trees.

Toward the end of the day they passed Michael Lupin, who was wrestling with a flat tire. "Need any help?" Joe called. Lupin merely scowled and waved them on.

Just before sunset the brothers broke out of the woods near the banks of a broad lake. The lake's placid waters reflected the emerald glory of the trees lining its shores. Half a mile ahead they spotted a big A-frame building with a line of docks in front of it.

"Fire Lake Lodge, dead ahead," Frank said.

"Beat you there," Joe replied, digging into his bike's pedals. The younger Hardy shot ahead momentarily; then Frank recovered from his surprise and sprinted after him.

Soon the two were racing neck and neck toward the lodge checkpoint, a long tentlike pavilion with a table across the front. A helicopter sat on a wide swath of lawn behind the tent, and several cameras were set up near the table.

Vince Bennett stood next to the table, all smiles. He called to the brothers as they hit the brakes and skidded to a stop.

"Looks like a tie to me," Bennett said. "Whoa! Watch out." He backed up as Michael Lupin braked in right beside the brothers.

"Never count the old man out," Lupin said, a slight grin cracking his bearded face.

"Good to see you, Michael," Bennett said. "You, too, Frank and Joe. Hey, Joe, I thought we lost you at the bottom of the mountain. Great comeback. Great footage, too. The race sponsors are gonna eat that up. It'll look super on TV."

"I wasn't thinking of TV when my brakes failed," Joe said, a bit peeved.

"Of course you weren't," Bennett said. "And I don't mean to imply that you shouldn't be more careful in the future. I don't want anyone hurt in this race. But danger's part of the game, isn't it?"

"Danger's part of life," Lupin interjected. "Check me through. I want to get some grub and take a shower."

"I'll leave you to it, then," Bennett said. "Don't forget to check your kayaks and other equipment tonight." He turned and walked toward the helicopter.

The race officials quickly processed Lupin and the Hardys, giving them room assignments and tentative starting times. All three checked their bikes into the equipment rack, where their support crews would pick them up later. Then they headed for the lodge. As the three competitors walked, Frank said, "Nice sprint at the end there, Mr. Lupin. You nearly caught us."

Lupin almost smiled. "I'd have been here long ago if I hadn't blown that tire on a sharp stick. You boys did pretty well, too—considering your early setback."

31

"We're in this for the long haul," Joe said.

"Yeah," Lupin replied. "Me, too. I don't like quitters. I'd better check my hired crew. They should be okay, but . . . well, they're not my regular trainer." He turned left at the A-frame, heading for a smaller building marked Support.

Joe and Frank entered the high-ceilinged lodge and quickly found their rooms. Jamal and Chet were hanging out, waiting for them.

"Glad you both made it," Jamal said.

"When we saw the mountain footage, we had our doubts," Chet added.

"Just a little sabotage with my brakes," Joe said. "Nothing to worry about."

"Sabotage?" Jamal and Chet said simultaneously.

"Someone loosened the cable grips," Frank said. "Though we can't imagine why."

"To make the race more exciting?" Chet suggested. "Joe looked great on TV."

"That's pretty extreme," Jamal said. "I know the resort wants big publicity, but Joe could have been seriously hurt."

"And that kind of publicity they *don't* need," Joe said. "We'll just have to double check all the equipment from now on."

"There's not much you can sabotage on a kayak," Jamal said.

"We'll still need to be careful," Frank replied.

"Are you guys hungry?" Chet asked.

"Famished," Joe said. "Give me and Frank time for a quick shower and we'll hit the dining hall."

Dinner was an informal affair, with many competitors just grabbing some food and heading for their rooms. With two nights of camping out ahead, everyone wanted to get a good night's sleep.

Though it was difficult to count with people drifting in and out, it seemed to the Hardys that the field had thinned a bit already. After eating, Frank and Joe decided to check on their kayaks, while Chet and Jamal went to pack away the mountain bikes.

"Don't worry," Jamal said. "We'll have 'em street legal by the time we see you in St. Esprit."

"And we'll double check the brakes," Chet added.

"Great," Frank said. "See you back inside in a couple of minutes."

Night had fallen while the Hardys were inside, and a pale half-moon was just peeking above the trees on the lake's eastern shore. Big floodlights lit the boathouse near the docks, though the farthest slips remained in shadow.

The brothers checked in with the boathouse guard, went inside, and gave their kayaks the once-over. The small, sleek vessels and double-sided paddles seemed to be in perfect working condition.

"No brakes to sabotage on these," Joe said.

Frank nodded and the two of them headed back toward the lodge. Light flooded through the big windows at the front of the A-frame, and shadows of the people within danced across the lawn outside.

"Beautiful night," Frank said, taking a deep breath of the cool air.

Joe nodded. "Too bad we have to hit the hay early."

As they neared the side door, though, the sounds of angry voices from around the corner caught the brothers' attention.

"Ssh!" hissed a woman's voice. "Do you want someone to hear?" The conversation continued after that but in lower tones. The brothers couldn't make out the words.

Frank and Joe exchanged a glance. Both of them crept around the side of the building toward the voices. The back corner of the lodge came almost to the edge of the woods. The Hardys stopped at the bend and listened.

A deep, masculine voice drifted around the corner. Even whispering, its tones carried through the night air.

"What we need," the voice said, "is to put some of the contestants *out* of the race."

4 Water, Water, Everywhere

Anger flared in Joe's eyes. He was about to charge around the corner to confront the conspirators, but Frank put his hand across Joe's chest. The older Hardy put a finger to his lips, indicating that they should both keep silent.

"What do you mean?" a female voice said warily.

"I'm just saying," the deep voice replied, "that accidents happen all the time in this kind of race."

"He's right," another male voice said. "The fewer racers, the better chance we have to come out on top."

"You're both crazy," the woman replied. "If we're caught cheating, that's end of the race—the end of everything. We might just as well shoot ourselves in the foot."

"I'm willing to do that," the deep voice said, "if it'll bring us the publicity we need."

"You've been watching too much TV," the woman said. "Do you think that *any* publicity is *good* publicity? Well, I don't buy it. I'm running this team, and we're going to play it my way. If any of you don't agree, you can quit. I promise I won't miss you."

Frank and Joe cautiously edged to the corner of the building and peered around. In the back, near a service door, stood a woman and two men. Dark shadows covered all of them. In the distance a light shone from the lodge's parking lot.

One of the men was tall and large, bigger than Chet. The other—a skinny man with long hair—leaned against the handlebars of a mountain bike. Despite the dim light, the brothers recognized the woman as Kelly Hawk.

"Kelly," the big man with the deep voice said, "there's a lot at stake here—more than just you and your rep."

"Too much to risk by cheating," Kelly Hawk snapped. "How are you going to do our people any good by messing with this race? Don't you think I can win on my own?"

The big man dug the toe of his boot into the ground. "I didn't mean it that way, Kelly," he said.

"Of course we think you can win," the thin man said. "But it would be better if it were a sure thing. If you won, people would *have* to pay attention to our cause."

"Not if I won by cheating," Kelly replied. "Cheating would bury us quicker than a herd of bulldozers. And think of the shame to our families, our friends, our nation if anyone found out."

She looked from one of the men to the other, her eyes gleaming in the darkness. "I couldn't live with myself if I cheated, and I won't have you two cheating on my behalf. Do I make myself clear?"

The men nodded slowly and said, "Yes, Kelly."

"Good. Now, load my bike into the van and catch some rest. I need everything in top condition for the road race stage. I need both of you thinking clearly, too. Don't do anything stupid, understand?"

The men nodded again. "Yes, Kelly."

"Okay, scram," she said. "I'm going to turn in."

The two men turned and walked toward the parking lot, taking the bike with them. Kelly sighed and shook her head. She tried to go in through the service door, but it was locked. Frustrated, she kicked the door with her boot.

"Any trouble back here?" Frank asked. He stepped from the shadows with Joe right behind him.

Kelly jumped. "Whoa! Don't sneak up on a girl like that!"

"We heard arguing," Joe said, "and thought we'd better check."

A wry smile cracked Kelly's lips. "You two are real Boy Scouts, aren't you?"

"Just concerned citizens," Frank said.

"Well, this doesn't concern you," she replied.

"It does if someone is trying to sabotage the race," Joe said. "Some competitors will do anything to win."

Kelly's dark eyes narrowed. "How long were you two lurking around that corner?"

"Long enough to hear what you said to those men," Frank replied. "It sounds like they want to make trouble."

"John and Jim?" she said. "They just talk big. Look, you two, I'm in this race to win publicity for my people and our cause, I told you that before. You think I'm going to let a couple of goons screw that up?"

"It sounded like they might have ideas of their own," Joe replied.

"I can handle them, believe me," Hawk said. "You worry about *your* support team, I'll worry about *mine*. Now, if you don't mind, I need to catch some rest. Don't bother walking me 'home,' I can find my own way." She pushed past them and headed for the lodge's main entrance.

Joe and Frank watched her go. Then Joe said, "What do you think?"

"She seems sincere," Frank replied. "We'll have to keep a careful lookout, though."

"And double check our equipment every day."

Frank nodded. "Come on. Let's get some sleep."

The aches and pains of the previous day's ride had ebbed somewhat by the time the Hardys woke the next morning. They ate a quick breakfast and headed down to the boathouse to check over their equipment. They saw no sign of Kelly Hawk or her crew, but many of the other racers were down near the docks. Frid, Collins, and Curtis spent some time talking to their hired support team before checking their kayaks.

The Clemenceaus spent as much time talking to the media as making preparations for the race. Roger Baldwin and Michael Lupin kept to themselves, preparing diligently and going through calisthenics routines.

"If you look up *intense* in the dictionary, you'll find pictures of those two," Chet said.

"They're not alone in this crowd," Jamal remarked, looking around. "Some folks are taking this race *very* seriously."

"Let's hope that no one is taking it seriously enough to purposely cause trouble," Joe said.

"Don't worry," Jamal said. "After what you told us last night, we'll keep a close watch on Kelly Hawk's crew."

"Thanks, guys," Frank said. "Let's give these boats one more look over and then check in for the race."

Starting times for the day were based on the finish times turned in on the previous day's race. The long, broad nature of Fire Lake would give those in the back of the pack a good chance to catch up with the leaders. Fire Creek, the winding river beyond the lake, would present fewer opportunities, even without the hazards of its rapids and whitewater.

Because the kayak race led directly into the hiking portion of the Speed Times Five Adventure Race, the competitors had to pack enough supplies to last them until they reached civilization once more.

At the staging area, Maggie Collins was having trouble stowing all of her gear in her kayak.

"Need some help?" Joe offered.

The young coed almost jumped at the sound of his voice. "Oh! No, thank you," she said. "I can manage it. Thanks for offering."

Quentin Curtis, one of the other students, came over from where he'd been working on his own kayak. "Hey, Maggie," he said, "let me give you a hand with that."

She smiled at him. "Yeah, hey, thanks," she said. Robert Frid came over as well. Working together, the three of them quickly solved the problem.

Joe walked away and said to Frank, "I guess it was just *my* help she didn't need."

Frank shrugged. "Well, we *are* competitors—even if you and I are cooperating, and she and her two friends are working together."

"At some point," Jamal said, "despite all this friendliness, *someone* has to win this race."

Joe smiled. "And that person is gonna be *me.*"

"Not if I get there first," Frank replied.

"Well, now that we've got *that* settled . . ." Chet said.

The four friends hauled the Hardys' kayaks to their starting positions. Frank and Joe said so long to Chet and Jamal. The Hardys wouldn't be seeing their support crew for two days, until all of them were scheduled to meet at the St. Esprit checkpoint. Then Frank and Joe took their places and all four of them waited for the Hardys' turn to start.

Despite their troubles on the mountain section of the course, the Hardys' times put them into the thick of the race. Roger Baldwin was slightly ahead of them, as were the three college students—Frid, Curtis, and Collins. Michael Lupin would hit the water right after the brothers did.

Georges and Victoria Clemenceau had a position at the front of the field, with Kelly Hawk close behind. All three of the front-runners were nearly halfway across the lake by the time the Hardys left the starting gates.

"We've got a lot of time to make up," Frank noted as they left the docks.

"Then we'd better get moving," Joe said. He dug in hard with his double-sided paddle and shot forward. Frank quickly caught up with his brother and they jockeyed for position as they skimmed across Fire Lake's placid water.

The brothers made good time, gaining on the leaders and leaving many of the slower racers behind. Much of the competition seemed to be falling away now, with only the best racers maintaining their distance from the pack.

Looking ahead, Joe saw that the Clemenceaus had lost much of their lead. "Kelly Hawk looks like she might pass them," Joe said to Frank.

The older Hardy nodded. "I read in the paper that

this isn't the Clemenceaus' best leg of the event," he said. "They're more road and trail athletes."

"The college students seem to be doing okay," Joe noted.

"We'll catch them shortly after we hit the river, I'm betting," Frank said. "Baldwin's fallen back a bit, too. We might be able to pass him as well." He glanced over his shoulder. "But Lupin's right on our tails."

"We'll just have to shake him, then," Joe said, digging in harder.

As they neared the far shore, they passed a kayak that had sprung a leak and was foundering in the chilly water. The race water patrol had the incident under control, but Joe shot Frank a suspicious glance. Both were wondering if it could have been sabotage.

Another contestant was hung up on the rocks at the entrance to Fire Creek. Again, race officials had the situation well in hand, and the Hardys paddled by into the next part of the course.

Fire Creek was much larger and rougher than its name implied. The river ran swiftly as it left the lake, and both brothers had to work hard to keep the current from pushing them into the rocks lining either shore.

"Yeehoo!" Joe shouted.

"Better swing that paddle, or this is gonna be a mighty short trip," Frank replied with a grin. "If I remember the maps right, the rapids come up pretty quick."

True to Frank's memory, the river rounded a bend and plunged downhill. Rocks like the backs of huge turtles sprang up from the riverbed, churning the water into white foam.

The chilly liquid tossed the kayaks one way, then another. Frank and Joe paddled furiously, trying to avoid the rocks and have a clean run to the next calm stretch of the river.

Frank banged his paddle against a submerged rock and nearly lost his grip. He snagged the other end of his paddle just before it toppled out of his reach. As he regained his composure, he saw Roger Baldwin and the college students navigating the waters ahead.

Roger Baldwin was in the lead, paddling strong and true, avoiding the rocks and hidden obstacles. Quentin Curtis, pulling hard, had nearly caught up to Baldwin. Robert Frid was making a good go of it, though his kayak skidded dangerously close to some of the rocks.

Maggie Collins, though, was struggling against the rough water near the far shore. The riverbank had risen on either side of Fire Creek, and both shores were lined with treacherous rocks. Powerful currents tugged at Collins's small vessel. She spun around backward.

Before Frank could even shout a warning, the stern of her kayak smacked into a boulder. The boat flipped over and the white water sucked Maggie Collins under.

5 Rapidly Deteriorating

"Joe!" Frank called, pointing to the upside-down kayak. He paddled toward Collins's overturned boat.

"Maybe she'll right herself," Joe yelled back, following his brother toward the far side of the river. "Any decent kayaker knows how to flip back over."

"In this current, she may not be able to!" Frank replied. He paddled hard to where Maggie Collins's boat was caught in the churning water.

"Hey!" Joe called. "Help here! We need some help!" The roar of the rapids nearly drowned out the sound of his voice, and Joe wondered whether anyone other than Frank could hear him.

Robert Frid was the closest to them. He turned and came to help as well. His teammate Quentin Curtis was farther away. Curtis kept going, though, and the Hardys couldn't be sure whether he'd heard their cry for help. A bit farther up the river, they saw Roger Baldwin turn and begin the arduous task of paddling upstream toward them.

Frank arrived at the overturned kayak first. The small boat was pinned against some half-submerged rocks by the rushing current. Frank reached out with his paddle and tried to pry up the edge of Collins's sleek kayak.

The force of the water was too strong. It was all Frank could do to keep from being crushed up against the rocks as well.

"Let me help," Joe offered, maneuvering in beside his older brother. The Hardys had done some tandem kayaking before, but the raging water made this a far trickier operation.

Stowing their paddles would have left them at the mercy of the river, so lifting with their hands seemed out of the question. Together, they used their paddles to try to rock the kayak back over. The surging river made it impossible, though. Despite their efforts, the white water shoved the brothers' kayaks up against the submerged boat.

"If we don't break this logjam, she'll drown for sure!" Joe said. He spotted Michael Lupin racing down toward them from upstream. "Hey! Help!" Joe called, but Lupin shot by, sparing only a short glance. "That rat!" Joe fumed.

"Hold my kayak," Frank replied. "I'm going in." He stowed his paddle and wriggled out of his kayak's seat just as Robert Frid reached them from downstream. Frank saw Roger Baldwin coming to their aid as well, but he knew he couldn't afford to wait. He grabbed the edge of Collins's kayak and jumped overboard.

As Frank hit the cold, rushing water, he heard Frid call, "How can I help?" The roar of the river crushed Joe's reply.

Even holding onto the edge of the kayak, Frank had to struggle to avoid being swept away by the river. Whitewater dashed all around him, making it nearly impossible to move. He braced his feet against the rock next to Collins's kayak and pushed. No good.

Taking a deep breath, he dove under the water. It seemed like forever since Maggie Collins had first submerged, but she was still conscious, still struggling; her legs had gotten caught inside her boat.

Frank reached out and tried to grab her hands. But she was flailing so wildly that he only brushed her fingertips. Something bumped into his side, and Frank almost lost his breath.

Turning, he saw that someone else had jumped into the water next to him. Frank knew it wasn't Joe, but through the turbulence he couldn't make out who it was. The older Hardy and the stranger both reached for Maggie Collins, and this time, they got a good grip.

With one rescuer pulling on each of her hands, they freed the young coed from the overturned kayak. Maggie Collins and Frank broke the surface simultaneously. Collins gasped for air and grabbed the side of her upside-down boat; she looked exhausted. A moment later Roger Baldwin surfaced beside them.

Looking around, Frank saw that Joe still had hold of his boat and Robert Frid was holding Baldwin's. Both were struggling to avoid drifting downstream.

"Th-thanks," Maggie Collins sputtered.

"Is your boat okay?" Baldwin asked. "Let's flip it over and get you back in the race."

"Wait," Joe said. "She may need medical attention."

"No," Collins replied. "I'm fine. I just need a few moments to recover."

Frank nodded. "Okay, one . . . two . . . three . . . heave!" He, Collins, and Baldwin pushed. Without the coed's extra weight holding it down, they righted the kayak easily.

As soon as the boat flipped, Maggie Collins scrambled back into the seat. Her paddle was attached to the boat by a tether, and she picked it up immediately. The impetus of the rescue carried her kayak out of the pack and back toward the middle of the course.

With Collins's boat off the rocks, the other kayaks began to move as well. Baldwin quickly grabbed the side of his boat and slid aboard. The Hardys weren't so lucky.

With the other boats no longer blocking them, they slipped toward the rocks that had trapped

Maggie Collins. Frank lost his footing and went under. The whitewater pushed him under, and his head banged against a boulder. Fortunately, his racing helmet saved him from any injury.

He popped up again, and Joe grabbed his arm. "Hang on, Frank!" Joe called. "We need some help here!" But the other racers were too far downstream, battling the current once more.

Another racer shot past heading downstream, too caught up in the challenges of the course to stop.

Frank and Joe struggled while their kayaks bumped up against the rocks. Finally, the older Hardy scrambled back aboard. With Frank out of the water, the brothers' years of kayaking experience took over, and they soon pushed themselves free of the rocks.

"That was a close one!" Joe said as they headed downstream once more.

"About three different times," Frank added, deftly wiping the water from his brow with his sleeve as he paddled.

They shot through another section of rapids and then entered a calmer section of water. As they did, they saw the racer who had passed them scrambling ashore, a broken paddle in her hand. She tugged her boat behind her but didn't seem to be in any real distress.

"This part of the course will probably cut down the competition a bit," Frank said.

"Just so long as *we* aren't the part it cuts down," Joe replied.

At the next bend in the river, far ahead now, they saw Collins, Frid, and Baldwin still traveling in a tight pack.

"We can catch them if we push hard," Joe said. "I don't think they're as good at kayaking as we are."

"We'll need a lead going into the bike stage if we want to have any chance to place in the rankings," Frank said. "Baldwin and the Clemenceaus are sure to be tough on the road."

"I'd like to catch that Lupin guy, too," Joe said angrily. "He could have stopped and helped, but he didn't."

"There's no rule that you have to help your competition," Frank replied. "C'mon, let's make up some distance." He and Joe dug in hard, and their kayaks slowly began to close the gap to the other racers.

By late afternoon they had passed Collins, Frid, and Baldwin once more. They saw several other racers stranded on the side of the river, but no one seemed in need of rescue, so the brothers pushed on.

They never did catch sight of Lupin again, but by the time the checkpoint came into view, they could see Quentin Curtis just ahead of them. He glanced back at the brothers as he paddled wearily toward shore.

The brothers beached their kayaks and recorded their times with the checkpoint officials just after Curtis. "Have you seen Maggie and Robert?" Curtis asked, peering upstream.

"We just passed them," Frank said. "They should be in any minute."

As he spoke, Collins and Frid appeared at the top of the bend and headed toward the checkpoint landing. Curtis let out a long sigh of relief.

Joe seemed about to say something, but Frank put his hand on his brother's shoulder. "Let's grab some grub from our boats," Frank said. Joe nodded but glanced from Curtis to Collins, and a spark of anger flashed in his blue eyes.

The Hardys walked the short distance from the checkpoint station back to their kayaks. Sealed in watertight bags, their food had survived the river in fine shape. As they hauled out their provisions and blankets, Collins and Frid beached their kayaks and headed to the checkpoint station. A few minutes later Roger Baldwin did the same.

"Hey," Joe called to him, "thanks for helping back there."

Baldwin gave a curt nod. "Don't mention it."

While Baldwin hiked toward the check-in station, the brothers headed for the camping area. Though it wasn't dark yet, some of the other competitors had already built a large fire.

"That fire'll feel mighty good," Frank said, still wet from rescuing Collins. He and Joe took up spots near the blaze and opened their food pouches.

Kelly Hawk, the Clemenceaus, and a number of other competitors were seated around the fire nearby. Hawk sat stoically, staring into the fire. The

50

Clemenceaus, though, were cooking a very tasty-looking meal—chicken in a white sauce with vegetables—in an aluminum pan with a folding handle.

"How can you eat that?" Victoria Clemenceau asked, eyeing the Hardys' freeze-dried fare.

Joe frowned. "It's edible, it's light, it's easy to carry," he said. "Doesn't carting all that extra stuff slow you down?"

"Perhaps," Georges Clemenceau replied, "but it is worth it."

"Just because the conditions are barbaric, doesn't mean we must eat like barbarians," Victoria added.

Those gathered around the fire laughed, even Kelly Hawk. As the laughter died away, the sounds of another conversation drifted to the Hardys' ears.

"I don't care how far ahead you were," Maggie Collins said, "you should have come back. We're in this together, aren't we?"

"Sure we are," Quentin Curtis replied sheepishly. "But there was nothing I could do—honestly."

"Quent would have helped if he could have," Robert Frid said. "Don't forget, though, we need to keep our eyes on the prize here."

"C'mon," Curtis said. "This isn't the place to discuss this. Let's take a walk down the riverbank." The three of them turned and walked away.

"Well," Joe whispered to Frank, "at least Curtis isn't getting off scot-free. I wish I could say the same of that Lupin guy. He should have stopped to help. Where is he, anyway?"

Frank shrugged. "I saw his kayak on the shore when we landed. He must be off by himself somewhere."

By the time darkness fell, the riverbank camp was crowded with competitors. Many had not made the checkpoint cut-off by dark and would therefore be out of the race. Race rules required that there could be no boating after dark, and so the disqualified racers were forced to camp upstream—in less comfortable conditions than the checkpoint camp.

The camera crews and race officials had a nice tent city higher up the riverbank, but the contestants were responsible for their own accommodations. Most of the racers had brought warm blankets in waterproof bags; the Clemenceaus and a few others had brought sleeping bags.

Joe and Frank bedded down in blankets by the fire, glad to have made the cut. Slumber took the brothers quickly. They slept soundly until the noise of a helicopter woke them the next morning, just before dawn.

"That must be Bennett," Kelly Hawk said, yawning. She rose from her spot near the fire and stretched. "He likes to keep tabs on his racers, but he's not much for sleeping under the stars."

Sure enough, as Joe and Frank roused themselves, they saw Vince Bennett working his way through the camp—camera crew in tow—talking to the remaining racers.

"Ugh," Joe said. "I'm in no mood to be on TV this morning."

"Me neither," Frank said, stretching a kink out of his neck. "Let's go check the boats before we eat."

"Good idea."

The brothers packed away their blankets and headed to the riverbank, where the kayaks lay beached. They found Michael Lupin crouched over his boat, working on something in the semi-darkness.

"Hey, Lupin," Joe said. "Why didn't you stop to help us yesterday?"

Lupin stood and scowled at the brothers. "This is a *race*," he said. "I'm in it to win, not to help other competitors."

"There's also a fair play and safety rule," Frank said. "Not to mention common courtesy."

"There's also a rule about interfering with other racers and teams," Lupin replied. "And I heard that you two pressed your luck on that point. Don't expect me to be disqualified, even if *you* want to be."

"Who said we were going to be disqualified?" Joe asked, his eyes narrowing with anger.

"Everyone in camp knows it," Lupin said. "Except maybe you two. If you're smart, you'll keep to yourselves from now on—assuming Bennett doesn't bounce you out before we start today." He walked away but called back, "See you at the starting line—maybe."

Joe stepped forward, fists clenched, but Frank said, "Let it go, Joe. He's not worth it."

"That guy really steams me," Joe said. "I see why he got voted off that TV show."

"Let's check our gear and then get our start times for the day," Frank said.

The brothers checked out the kayaks and stowed their gear inside them. Then they hiked up the bank toward the officials' tent.

Just before they reached it, though, someone called, "Hey, you two, stop!"

6 Not Just Another Walk in the Woods

The Hardys spun and saw a man walking toward them out of the darkness. Though he didn't have his usual camera crew in tow, the brothers quickly recognized Vince Bennett, the race organizer.

"I've been looking for you Hardy boys," Bennett said.

"What can we do for you, Mr. Bennett?" Frank asked.

"I heard what you did yesterday," Bennett said. "You know, of course, that your actions were not strictly according to race rules."

"Here it comes," Joe whispered apprehensively.

"However," Bennett continued, "your actions were in the spirit of fair sportsmanship and may very well have saved Ms. Collins's life. Therefore, I commend you. This is the kind of thing the sponsors and I want people to remember when they think of the Speed Times Five Adventure Race. If you're willing, my camera crew would like to interview you on the subject."

"We're not big on publicity," Frank said.

"We did what we did because it was the right thing to do," Joe added.

Bennett nodded his understanding. "Yeah. Okay. I thought you might say something like that. If you change your minds, though, just let me know."

"We will," Frank said.

"On to other business, then," Bennett said. "I was talking to your support crew last night, Jamal and . . ." He paused, trying to recall the name.

"Chet," Joe said.

"Right, Chester," Bennett continued. "They tell me that you're good at spotting trouble and that you've worked with law enforcement in the past. Now, I don't want to say that I'm concerned about the race, but something feels a bit funny to me. I could definitely use a few more eyes down at ground level. You'd be surprised what you can miss from a helicopter, or even from our course cameras."

"And you want us to do what?" Frank asked.

"Just keep an eye on things," Bennett said. "Give me a ring on the emergency phones if you see anything funny going on. That way my people can get right on it."

"We can do that," Joe said.

Bennett grinned. "Great. I appreciate it. Good luck in the race. And remember, play fair and stay safe."

"Don't worry, we will," Frank said.

The brothers finished their trek to the officials' tent and got their morning start times. Then they ate breakfast and prepared to go.

Georges Clemenceau was first into the river that morning, followed by Kelly Hawk, and then Victoria Clemenceau and a few other top racers. Because he'd passed them the previous day, Michael Lupin started ahead of the brothers, as did Quentin Curtis. After the Hardys came Maggie Collins, Robert Frid, Roger Baldwin, and the rest of the pack.

The morning sky shone deep blue over the racers as they navigated the treacherous white water. As midday approached, the Hardys passed several half-sunken boats with soggy racers clinging to them. No one seemed to be in any danger, though, and race officials were already on the scene.

The brothers beached at the final river checkpoint just before noon. Chet and Jamal met them by the landing site and resupplied the Hardys with provisions for the next part of the journey. Joe and Frank completed their checkpoint rituals quickly. They changed into dry shoes, strapped packs on their backs, and hiked off into the forest.

They'd made good time during the morning and had drawn closer to the front of the pack. Chet and

Jamal told them that Hawk and the Clemenceaus were still among the race leaders, with Michael Lupin close behind. Roger Baldwin had made up time, too, and zipped through the checkpoint. He entered the woods just before the Hardys.

"With his triathlon training, he'll be really tough in this phase and the next," Frank said.

"The hiking and bike racing are strong points for the Clemenceaus, too," Joe replied. "If we want to have any kind of decent ranking at the end, we'll need to keep close to all of them."

The course cut through the forest over beautiful rolling hills. The trail was clearly marked with a good, firm dirt surface. Still, the brothers had a long trek ahead of them to the evening's checkpoint.

The hike claimed its share of victims, too. They passed a woman with a sprained ankle and, later, a man who'd apparently stumbled into a nest of wasps. Both contestants were talking with race officials via their emergency phones, and neither seemed to be in serious distress.

The Hardys caught up with Quentin Curtis early in the afternoon. He was jogging fairly slowly and waved as the brothers passed him by.

"He doesn't look too winded," Frank said.

"Maybe he's waiting for his friends," Joe replied as he and Frank jogged over the next hill.

"I guess the woods can be dangerous if you're running alone," Frank said.

As if to prove his words, twenty minutes later the brothers topped a rise and nearly ran into a bull moose. The huge animal walked slowly beside the trail, browsing new green shoots off the branches within its reach. The animal's dark eyes spotted the brothers and its big nostrils flared.

Frank and Joe stopped dead in their tracks. The moose stood only a few feet from the trail, effectively blocking their path.

"Can we leave the trail and cut around it?" Joe whispered.

"According to the rules, yes," Frank whispered back. "We'll lose some time, though."

"I'd rather lose some time than try to face down a moose," Joe replied. "Let's back up and cut over to the right."

"Check."

Carefully edging backward the brothers soon reached the top of the ridge. The moose eyed them as they went but kept browsing the foliage.

Keeping the animal just in sight, the brothers left the trail and followed the ridge line for several hundred yards. Then they cut back down into the small moraine, paralleling the marked path.

Their scout training stood the Hardys in good stead as they moved through the woods. They soon cut back to the main trail, well past where they'd seen the moose.

"Whew!" Joe sighed. "I guess we'll have to be noisier as we go—give the local fauna plenty of warning that we're coming."

"Good idea," Frank said. "I'd rather keep to the main trail if we can. It may be legal to leave the path, but they've designed the course so that any deviation will cost the contestants time."

"Well, if the moose stays there, he'll hold up all the other racers, too," Joe said.

Frank nodded as he jogged. "I wonder if anyone in front of us had to leave the trail."

"I was too busy watching the moose to look for other contestants," Joe replied.

"Me, too. We should call the moose hazard in, though."

"Good idea," Joe replied. He pulled out his emergency radiophone and relayed the information about the moose to the race control center. A moment later both their radios flared to life with a warning broadcast to all contestants.

"There we go helping the competition again," Frank said.

Joe laughed. "Yeah. Maybe Michael Lupin will want us kicked out because of it."

"That guy would be better off if he channeled more of his aggression into running," said Frank.

"I'd say he's doing pretty well on that," Joe countered. "We haven't passed him yet."

"Or Baldwin, either," Frank said. "Come on, let's push it a bit to see if we can catch someone."

As the afternoon wore on, the terrain grew more difficult, turning from rolling wooded hills into rocky valleys and steep ridges. They passed several other contestants, but saw no sign of Baldwin, Lupin, or the leaders.

"Tonight's checkpoint can't be far," Frank said as the sun sank toward the western horizon.

"Good thing, too," Joe replied. "I'm beat. These rocky trails are murder on the knees."

"Just wait until the real climbing starts tomorrow," Frank said.

"Bring it on," Joe said, wiping the sweat from his brow.

Less than half an hour later they jogged into the midleg checkpoint. They visited the officials' tent and registered their times.

"How are we doing?" Frank asked.

"Pretty well," an official with the nametag Sullivan said. "Only about a dozen in front of you."

"Any more dropouts?" Joe asked.

"A couple of sprained ankles in the group ahead of you," Sullivan said, "and three more behind. Plus, one got skunked. The rest of you will want to give him a wide berth during the rest of the race. We don't have enough water to wash him down properly."

"Maybe the Clemenceaus brought some tomato juice," Joe offered with a smile.

Sullivan and the brothers laughed.

The Hardys quenched their thirst from the race officials' fresh water supply and then refilled their canteens. The contestants ahead of them had already started a big campfire in a clearing, and a number of racers sat gathered around it. Kelly Hawk, Victoria Clemenceau, and Michael Lupin sat by the fireside. As the Hardys settled in and ate some food from their packs, Roger Baldwin jogged up from the officials' tent. He grunted an acknowledgment to the other racers, then took a place by the fire and ate.

"I don't remember passing him," Joe whispered to Frank.

"We didn't pass Georges Clemenceau or Quentin Curtis, either," Frank replied, "but they're not here. Maybe we missed them during our moose detour."

"Could be," Joe said. "We weren't in the woods that long, but I suppose they could have taken their own detours."

"Or maybe they're just in some other part of the camp," Frank said. He smiled. "Maybe Georges is the one who got skunked."

Joe chuckled, but both he and Frank noticed that Victoria kept glancing back toward the officials' tent. As the sun sank, she got up and began to pace back and forth at the edge of the camp.

Joe leaned over to Kelly Hawk. "Where's Georges?" he asked.

Kelly shrugged. "Victoria came in by herself," she said. "I haven't seen Georges. I guess they got separated in the woods."

Many other racers straggled in as the evening drew on. Quentin Curtis, Maggie Collins, and Robert Frid arrived within a short distance of each other. Still, there was no sign of Georges Clemenceau.

"If he was in trouble," Lupin said, "he'd use the radio."

"Unless he couldn't," Maggie Collins added.

As darkness covered the small camp, Victoria's pacing became more frantic. The stars peeked out in the clear, black sky overhead and nocturnal animals began their ritual songs. All the other contestants had been accounted for, and even the race officials seemed a bit worried.

Suddenly, without warning, Victoria Clemenceau sprinted off into the darkened woods. Her cries echoed through the night-shrouded trees.

"Georges! Georges! Where are you?"

7 A Rock and a Hard Place

"That's a stupid thing to do," Michael Lupin said, watching Victoria run into the woods. "There's no way she can find her brother without a light. She'll be lucky if she doesn't get totally lost."

As Victoria disappeared into the darkness, Frank and Joe grabbed the flashlights out of their backpacks and dashed after her. It didn't take them long to find her. She'd tripped over a tree limb near the edge of the woods and lay sprawled on a carpet of leaves.

Joe helped her to her feet. "Take it easy," he said. "It won't help your brother for you to go running into the woods."

"We'll get on the camp radio," Frank said. "Start a systematic search for him."

"I never should have gone ahead of him," Victoria said, rubbing her ankle. "We should have stuck together, even if it reduced our chances of winning."

"Don't blame yourself," Joe said. "We'll find your brother."

Victoria leaned on the brothers and limped a bit as they returned to camp. "Do not worry," she said. "I have only twisted it. It will be fine."

"Okay," Frank said. "But maybe you should leave the searching to other people."

"But Georges is my brother," Victoria said.

"We'll look for him as though he were our own brother," Joe assured her.

The camp was already organizing a search by the time they got back. Checkpoint official Sullivan was on the phone to race HQ, requesting assistance.

"They say they'll send a couple of choppers," Sullivan said. "We're checking with the event photographers, too—to see if they can give us a clue where Mr. Clemenceau might have disappeared to. It would help, Ms. Clemenceau, if you'd stay with us and give us some more information."

Victoria Clemenceau nodded. "Of course," she said, rubbing her twisted ankle.

"We'll organize some other racers," Frank said. "Trace back along the route to see if we can find him."

"I wouldn't recommend that," Sullivan said. "We don't want anyone else lost. Our people should be able to cover it."

"What if he's hurt?" Joe said. "Time could be essential. Don't worry about Frank and me. We're experienced."

"So am I," Kelly Hawk said, approaching the group. "I'll go with you. Three people can cover more ground than two."

"Great," said Frank. "Find another person and we can form two teams. Maybe Michael Lupin— he has the outdoor survival experience."

Kelly frowned but said, "Okay. I guess we can't be too choosy at this point." She sprinted off and quickly returned with Lupin in tow. Lupin didn't look too pleased at being drafted, but he didn't complain.

"The official search team will be taking the main trail," Frank said, having coordinated his plan with Sullivan while Kelly was gone. "If we stick to the woods on either side of the path, we should be able to hit the ground they're not covering. If any of us find him, we'll get on the horn and contact HQ."

"What if we don't find him?" Lupin asked.

Frank and Joe glanced toward Victoria Clemenceau, talking with the race team a short distance away.

"We'll find him," Joe said.

"Even though I'm helping out here," Lupin said, "I still want to win this race. I'll need time to rest before tomorrow's leg. I'm not staying out here all night."

"Did it occur to you that they may *cancel* the race if Georges isn't found?" Kelly said angrily.

Lupin frowned. "Well, no," he said sheepishly.

"Let's get going," Frank said. "The sooner we find Georges, the sooner we get back."

The official search crew set off down the trail, moving quickly but cautiously. Hawk and Lupin took the woods on the left-hand side, while the Hardys took the forest on the right.

Moving in the dark, they all quickly lost sight of the camp. Joe had a compass and a map of the route and used them to keep the Hardys on track. Frank kept the main trail and the search crew in sight as the brothers swept the woods for signs of Georges Clemenceau.

"Where could he be?" Joe asked after forty-five minutes of fruitless searching. "And why would he leave the path?"

"He might have run into an animal, like we did," Frank said. "Or he might have been trying for a shortcut." Radio checks told him the other searchers hadn't found anything, either. "We just have to keep looking."

As they trudged through the brush, the night grew darker and the foliage thicker. Animal eyes shone in the beams of their flashlights, but the creatures quickly flitted away into the darkness.

The brothers found several small game trails and, each time they did, tracked the trail back to the main path before resuming their original course. In the distance, they heard Hawk, Lupin, and the other searchers calling Georges's name.

Two hours into the search, Joe noticed some broken foliage at the edge of a game trail as they backtracked from the main path. Shining his flashlight through the brush, he saw a flash of red in the woods.

"Frank!" he called. "I see something."

The older Hardy looked where Joe indicated. "Too red to be leaves at this time of year," Frank said. "And it looks as though someone left the path here."

The brothers quickly followed the tracks toward the red object. "Georges and Victoria wear red uniforms," Frank noted.

"Oh, man! That looks like a body!" Joe said.

They sprinted the last few yards, ignoring the brush that scratched their arms and legs.

Georges Clemenceau lay on his face in a pile of leaves in the middle of the small trail. Frank knelt to check on him. "He's still breathing," Frank said, "but it looks like he's had a nasty crack on the head."

"What do you think hit him?" Joe asked. Looking around, he saw no low-lying branches or any other obvious obstacles.

"It doesn't matter. Get on the horn while I see what I can do for him." The brothers' first-aid and EMT training had served them well during their previous cases.

Joe pulled out his radio and called the other searchers. "We've found him," Joe said. "He's alive, but he's had a bad crack on his head." He checked the Global Positioning System display on the emergency phone and read off the coordinates to the searchers. Then he stowed the radio and shone his flashlight toward the main trail so the others could locate them. "They're sending a chopper," he said.

"The woods are too thick to land here," Frank replied. "We'll have to move him to the main trail."

"Let's wait," Joe said. "The main team has a portable stretcher. How's he doing?"

"I think he's got a concussion," Frank said, "but I can't tell how bad it is. He doesn't seem to have any broken bones, and his breathing is regular. That's good, anyway. Why do you think Georges left the main path?"

"He might have tried to use this trail as a short-cut," Joe said. "It fits the directions on the map."

"If he did, it was a bad choice," Frank replied.

The main rescue team arrived within fifteen minutes.

"We sent Hawk and Lupin back already," one of the rescuers said. "You boys should head back, too, if you're going to continue racing." She and her colleague quickly assembled the portable stretcher they'd been carrying in their backpacks.

"We'll stick with you until the helicopter comes," Frank said.

"After all," Joe added, "who needs sleep?"

The four of them put Georges on the stretcher, carried him back to the main trail, and then found a spot where the chopper could pick him up. They used their flashlights to signal the chopper pilot, and soon Georges was on his way to a local hospital.

One of the rescue teams went with Clemenceau. The other hiked back to camp with the Hardys. Even moving quickly, it still took them an hour and a half to get back.

"Not much shuteye tonight," Joe groaned.

"Suck it up, Hardy," Frank joked. "This is a race, not a vacation."

The brothers fell asleep almost as soon as they rolled themselves into their blankets.

As the racers assembled the next morning, the Hardys were surprised to see Victoria Clemenceau near the front of the pack.

"Georges would not want me to drop out just because he cannot continue," she said stoically, her twisted ankle wound in sports tape.

Vince Bennett had arrived by helicopter during the night, and he spoke to the racers before the start of the new leg.

"I'm sure you'll all be glad to hear that Georges Clemenceau is recovering from that nasty bump on his head," Bennett said. "This seems a good time to remind all of you of the importance of safety during the competition. I would recommend sticking to the official course route rather than blazing your own trails.

"And look out for one another, please. I'd like to thank the people who helped our searchers find Georges last night." He paused for some brief applause from the crowd. "Now, let's get racing!"

With that, the first group of racers sprinted into

the woods once more. Hawk, Clemenceau, Lupin, and a number of others took to the trails before the brothers, which gave the Hardys a bit of much-needed rest before they, too, set off.

The course grew steeper and rockier, and quickly entered an area of steep-sided ravines. The Hardys found themselves climbing nearly as much as they were hiking.

"We'll be hitting the rappelling section pretty soon," Joe said.

Frank nodded, too winded to say anything at that moment.

Because of the brothers' adventure the previous night, some of the other competitors began to catch up with them once more. Roger Baldwin and Robert Frid made a push in the late morning and passed the brothers just before a long rope climb up a cliff face.

Frank and Joe struggled up the ropes and found Kelly Hawk and a number of others resting at the top of the cliff. Hawk was talking animatedly to a camera crew covering the race. As the brothers caught their breath and drank some water, they listened.

"Just ahead," Kelly said, wiping the sweat from her brow, "you'll see the kind of thing my people object to. The ravaged forests are a clear indication that the stewardship of this land has been forsaken. This is one reason my people are asserting their ancient treaty rights." She stood. "Come on," she said to the camera people, "I'll show you."

As Hawk and the crew hiked off toward the next hillside, Joe said, "She's lost quite a bit of time."

"I think making her point is probably more important to her," Frank replied. "She'll still have time to catch up later."

"We will, too," Joe said, taking another drink of water. "I wonder what she was talking about, though."

A few minutes later the brothers started off again. Their legs and arms burned from the long days of exertion, but they knew the other racers were facing the same trouble.

"I can't wait to hit Montreal and sleep in a real bed," Joe said as they topped the shoulder of another rugged hill.

"Whoa," Frank said as they crested the ridge, "I guess *this* is what Hawk was complaining about."

Ahead lay a hillside nearly devoid of trees. The barren swath stretched from the shoulder where the Hardys stood, back up the hillside beyond, and then down to a forest in the valley below. Tire tracks marked the rocky slopes where the lumber had been hauled away. The vista was desolate and nearly as lifeless as the surface of the moon.

Joe scowled and spat the dust from his mouth. "They should make clear-cutting illegal," he said.

"Yeah," Frank said. "Let's send a donation to Hawk's cause when we get home. But first, we have to finish this race. C'mon."

Cautiously, he began to hike down the blasted landscape, his feet kicking loose small rocks and gravel. Joe did the same, trying not to slip on the uneven ground.

"Is that Hawk and the camera crew down below?" Joe asked, shielding his eyes from the afternoon sun.

Frank peered in that direction and spotted three figures at the edge of a forest in the valley below. "I think so," Frank said. "But I doubt they'll wait for us to catch up and find out."

Joe looked up into the clear blue sky. "Do you hear thunder?" he asked.

Frank looked around, his gaze settling on the hillside behind them. What he saw set his heart pounding.

"Landslide!" he shouted.

8 Running in Place

High up the slope behind the Hardys, the hillside moved. Small rocks tumbled over bare ground, shaking loose dirt and larger rocks. Those rocks shook loose still more, until the whole hillside slumped toward the ridge the Hardys had crossed just minutes before.

"Run!" Frank urged.

He and Joe took off downslope, their feet slipping on the barren ground. Behind them, a cloud of gray dust roared and grew to huge proportions.

Sparing a momentary glance back as he ran, Joe shouted, "Cut to the right! Try to get out of the slide's direct path!"

Frank and Joe ran to the right, all the while continuing their downward plunge. The brothers moved as fast as they could while still maintaining their footing. Both knew that a single slip could leave them buried under tons of dirt and rock.

The slide toppled the few trees remaining on the slope and tossed them forward like driftwood on a dusty sea. The roar of the landslide grew louder—a rocky monster hungry to devour the brothers.

"We're not going to make it!" Joe cried.

"Just keep running," Frank said. Glancing back, he spotted a tall tree trunk coasting atop the rubble like a boat. The tree was near the leading edge of the slide and close to where Joe and Frank were running. With luck, they could just make it. "Go for the tree, Joe!" he called. "Maybe we can ride this out!"

As the slide caught up with them, the brothers turned and leaped for the tree. Joe landed solidly on the trunk and grabbed hold with both hands. Frank, however, tripped over some hurtling scree. He landed half on the uprooted tree, with his legs and lower body dangling in the dust.

The speed of the slide threatened to pull him off the trunk and into the crashing rubble. Frank's fingers lost their grip on the rough bark. He slipped off.

Joe stabbed out and grabbed his brother's arms. Frank's feet bounced among the sliding rocks for a moment, then Joe pulled him atop the tree trunk.

Even aboard the tree, the Hardys' position was dangerous. The trunk swayed and reeled, threatening to flip over. Frank and Joe used all their balance and agility to stay with the trunk as the slide rushed downhill.

The forest in the valley loomed large before them even as the landslide slowed its descent. They hit the woods with a mighty crash and tumbled off their boatlike tree trunk just as the slide rumbled to a halt.

The Hardys rose to their feet, battered and bruised, but glad to be alive. A cloud of gray dust washed over them as the remains of the landslide settled to the ground.

"Phew!" Joe said, brushing the grit off his clothes. "I've heard of people surfing avalanches before, but not landslides."

"I'm glad it was more dust than rock," Frank said. "It was still a close call, though. We're lucky to escape with just a few scrapes and bruises." He coughed some of the dust from his lungs.

As the haze cleared from the forest, the sounds of shouting drifted through the trees. "Help! Help!"

Instantly forgetting their aches and pains, Frank and Joe ran through the rubble toward the sound. Ahead of them, they saw the three people they'd previously spotted near the bottom of the slope. Kelly Hawk and a cameraman were struggling to pull the other member of the TV camera crew out from under a fallen tree. The woman's legs were pinned by both the tree and a pile of small rubble from the landslide.

The brothers raced to the woman's side and began digging with their hands. Kelly Hawk regarded the Hardys with a look of wonder.

"I can't believe you two are alive," she said. "You must be the luckiest guys on earth."

"You're pretty lucky, too," Frank replied. "Any closer and this slide might have buried all three of you."

"We were getting a shot of the clear-cut," said the cameraman. "Kelly was telling us about the dangers of erosion. Then you topped the hill and . . ."

The woman under the rubble groaned.

"Hang on," Joe said. "We'll have you out in a minute. One of you should use the emergency phone. Warn them about the slide area, too."

The cameraman stopped tugging on the tree and phoned for assistance. As Frank, Joe, and Kelly Hawk lifted the tree off the woman, the sound of a chopper echoed over the hills. The cameraman pulled his coworker free and the Hardys did some quick first aid.

"I'm all right, really," the woman said groggily. "Just a little banged up."

"It's better if you don't move," Joe said. "The medics will be here in a moment."

The chopper set down a short way from the forest, at the edge of the slide. A few minutes later, the blue-suited LMP paramedics had the woman stabilized and packed into the chopper. The cameraman went with them as the helicopter lifted off once more.

As Kelly Hawk and the brothers watched the airlift leave, their emergency radios crackled to life.

"This is a warning to all racers," Bennett's voice said. "Conditions in grid 87-849 are hazardous and may lead to rock slides. Racers should proceed with extreme caution, travel in groups, and consider alternate routes." He repeated the message twice and then signed off.

"The race goes on," Frank said.

"There's no business like show business," Joe noted. As he spoke, he saw figures skidding down through the settling dust behind them. "Some people won't stop for anything."

Turning back, the brothers saw that Kelly Hawk was already hiking up the trail ahead of them.

"The pack is catching up," Frank said. "We'd better get moving."

He and Joe trudged out of the forest and jogged up the trail beyond. They kept Kelly Hawk in sight for a while, but she was fresher than the brothers and soon pulled away from them.

The afternoon wore on slowly and the air grew hot and muggy.

Much of the pack had caught up with the Hardys by the time they reached the final rappelling challenge. The brothers weren't the only ones running out of energy, though. Robert Frid fell behind the Hardys once more, and Roger Baldwin was just completing his rappelling when the brothers arrived.

The race trail came to an abrupt halt atop a hundred-and-fifty-foot cliff. Race officials waited to assure the safety of the contestants as they rappelled down the cliff face to the path at the bottom. Several racers sat at the top of the cliff, working up the energy to continue.

Joe and Frank had done similar events in X-games competitions before, and they breezed down the cliff face with no difficulty.

"Whew!" Joe said as they reached the bottom. "A nice change from hiking."

"But not a very long change," Frank said, indicating the dirt trail before them. The rolling hills were past them now and the path wound through the green forests toward their next checkpoint—St. Esprit.

The Hardys passed Baldwin in the woods and, as the sun sank toward evening, had their sights on Kelly Hawk once more.

"I'm glad we're not the only ones getting tired," Frank gasped.

Joe nodded, too winded to say anything.

A small tent city in a campground on the outskirts of St. Esprit slowly came into view. Kelly Hawk jogged wearily ahead of the brothers.

"Let's see if we can catch her," Joe suggested.

Frank nodded, and the two of them began to trot. Soon the trot turned into an all-out sprint as the brothers poured every ounce of their energy into a big finish.

Kelly Hawk glanced back when she heard the pounding of their footsteps behind her. She began to run as the brothers drew near. Soon the three of them were racing neck and neck for the checkpoint. Sweat drenched the bodies of all three competitors and their breathing came in short gasps.

With a final lean, Frank crossed the finish line first, followed by Hawk and then Joe. All three of them staggered to the checkpoint desk to register their times.

Kelly Hawk's support crew came racing in from the sidelines, bringing her a water bottle and letting her lean on them as she left the registration table. Chet and Jamal came right behind, pressing water into the Hardys' hands.

"Boy, you look beat!" Chet said.

"You don't know the half of it," Joe replied. He sipped his water and wiped the sweat from his forehead.

"We've got the tent set up and the bikes all ready for tomorrow's leg," Jamal said.

Frank nodded his approval and puffed out air.

"We've even got hot food," Chet added.

Joe put his arm around Chet's shoulder. "Now, *that* is the best news I've heard all day." Together, the four friends walked to where Chet and Jamal had set up camp.

"How far back in the pack are we?" Frank asked as Jamal served him some stew.

"You're in good shape," Jamal said. "Even the leaders didn't come in too much before you. Victoria Clemenceau and Michael Lupin are in that bunch. Then you guys and Hawk."

"I saw the college group and that triathlon guy coming in as we walked over here," Chet added.

Joe munched a mouthful of stew. "I guess surfing that rockslide saved us as much time as it cost us helping the camera crew," he said between chews.

"I wouldn't recommend it as a race tactic, though," Frank said, rubbing his bruises.

"The rappelling points served as bottlenecks, which helped you out, too," Jamal said. "They had safety crews for only a couple of lines at a time, which gave the slower racers a chance to catch up."

"A clever tactic to keep things interesting for the TV coverage," Chet noted.

"We make the local news lately?" Joe asked.

"Not much," Chet said. "The race gets some coverage, and they mentioned the rockslide you were in today. Mostly it's the usual stuff: trade problems, experimental medicines gone missing, a few police chases, a bear wandering into a resort."

"Quite a bit of stuff on Kelly Hawk's Native American group, too," Jamal added. "They've been on the news nearly every night, protesting."

"Not without cause," Frank said, "judging from the clear-cut we saw."

"They're causing quite a ruckus," Jamal said. "There've been some arrests."

Frank and Joe nodded, and the group ate in silence for a while as the Hardys tried to regain some of their strength. Night crept over the camp as they relaxed. Vince Bennett stopped by with a camera crew for a quick interview. The Hardys were polite but terse in their comments. The crew soon looked bored and Bennett motioned them to move on.

81

"I'll check with you boys later," the race coordinator said with a wink.

"Only if you catch us before bedtime," Joe said.

Frank sighed as the crew walked away. "Not the best interview we've ever given."

"We're tired," Joe replied. "Why don't we check over the bikes and then turn in."

"Good idea," Frank said. He and Joe got up.

"Want us to go with you?" Chet asked.

"Nah," Joe said. "Just make sure our sleeping bags are ready when we get back."

They all chuckled and the brothers headed toward the bike storage area.

The campground didn't have the same level of facilities as the Fire Creek Mountain lodge. The race crew had installed a number of bicycle racks in the wide empty area between the camp showers and the vending machines behind the registration building. The spot they'd chosen wasn't well lit— only a dim glow from the neighboring buildings illuminated the area.

Most of the other racers had retired for the evening. The bicycle rack was deserted save for a lone figure crouched over the bikes. The man worked quickly and quietly. A black ski mask obscured his features.

The dim light from the distant shower building reflected off the small wire cutters in the saboteur's right hand.

9 Collision Course

"Hey, you!" Joe called. He sprinted toward the saboteur and threw a punch at the man's head. The man ducked out of the way and swung the wire cutters at Joe's face.

Joe reeled back, almost running into Frank as the older Hardy charged forward. Frank spun out of Joe's way and launched into a martial arts kick.

Frank's kick caught the man in the right forearm, and the wire cutters flew from the saboteur's gloved hand. The man staggered back, then turned and hopped over the first bicycle rack.

The Hardys leaped after him. The saboteur cleared three racks in succession like an Olympic hurdler. The brothers charged right after him, but their jumps weren't as clean. Joe nearly got caught in the last rack, and Frank had to reach out to steady his brother.

The slip allowed the saboteur to open up a big lead on the Hardys. He disappeared into the shadows behind the registration building. Their legs aching, the Hardys sprinted after him.

"Which way did he go?" Joe asked as they skidded to a halt behind the structure. The building was a long log cabin camp office that Vince Bennett had pressed into service for the race crews. The surrounding woods crept up almost to the back of the building. The shadows under the boughs were black as night; those near the cabin were not much brighter. The brothers saw no sign of the saboteur.

"Let's split up and circle the building," Frank said. "Whistle if you see him."

Joe nodded and lit out to the right, while Frank circled left. They met by the vending machines in front of the building without finding anything.

Joe shook his fist in anger. "Whoever he was, he was quick and clever," Joe said ruefully.

"Maybe not clever enough," Frank replied, his brown eyes peering into the darkness toward the camping area. He pointed toward a figure moving away from them through the small sea of tents. "Let's go," he whispered.

Joe nodded and the two of them sprinted quietly toward the figure. It was hard to keep the man in sight among the darkened tents, but the Hardys quickly closed the distance. Frank motioned that they should circle around either side, and Joe nodded his agreement.

Cutting through the tents, they soon got in front of the man and stepped out simultaneously from either side. The man jumped back as the brothers popped out in front of him.

"Robert Frid," Joe said, recognizing the man by the light of the distant campfire. "What are you doing lurking around?"

"You almost scared me to death!" Frid said, clutching his chest theatrically. He was wearing a navy blue shirt and pants but no ski mask. His right pocket, though, bulged with an unseen object.

"What do you have in your pocket?" Frank asked.

Frid frowned at the older Hardy. "Popcorn. Not that it's any of your business. What are you guys doing skulking around?"

"Just a little security patrol," Joe said. "We found someone tampering with the bikes—and you're the only person we saw near the bike rack."

"I went to the vending machines," Frid said. He pulled a small bag of prepackaged popcorn out of his pocket and shook it at Joe. "See? Popcorn. Who appointed you two cops?"

Before the brothers could answer, Maggie Collins and Quentin Curtis arrived. "Hey, Bob," Quentin said, "did you get lost or something?"

"These guys are hassling me," Frid said. "They think I was messing with the bikes. Tell 'em I was with you before I went to get popcorn."

"He left us only a couple of minutes ago," Maggie Collins said.

"See?" Frid replied. "I didn't have time to go messing with any bikes."

Frank scratched his head. "Yeah, okay," he said. "Sorry for hassling you. C'mon, Joe."

"Why don't you guys get some rest?" Curtis said, his voice tinged with hostility. "You've already gotten into enough trouble for *two* races."

Joe nearly turned back to confront Frid, but Frank stopped his younger brother. "Just ignore it," Frank whispered. "Let's hit the showers and go to bed."

"Showers?" Joe said as they kept walking. "I don't know. I feel as though dirt is all that's holding my bruises together."

"I know what you mean," Frank said. "We also need to talk to Bennett before we turn in."

"It looks like another restless night." Joe sighed.

On their way, the brothers searched for the wire cutters the saboteur had dropped but couldn't find them.

"He must have doubled back and picked them up," Frank said.

"Frid would have had time to do that," Joe noted.

"Not that we could prove it," Frank added.

Despite their lack of solid evidence, the Hardys found Bennett and told him about the possible sabotage. The race organizer promised to look into the incident and to post a guard around the equipment areas. After the conversation, the brothers hit the showers and retired for the night.

They woke fairly late, as the race had a start time just before ten A.M. After a quick breakfast with Chet and Jamal, all four of them went to recheck the Hardys bikes.

The bike area was crowded with competitors, all checking their equipment. The hired race teams, in bright yellow jump suits, worked side by side with their racers. Medics in blue uniforms with LMP logos carefully looked over the competitors' scrapes and bruises. No one seemed very happy over the increased level of security and the extra work it entailed.

Bennett and a security crew moved among the racers, discreetly asking questions. The Hardys noticed that contrary to his usual routine, Bennett was staying far away from the TV cameras today.

While the Hardys worked, Frid, Collins, Curtis, and some of the other racers eyed the brothers suspiciously.

"Nothing like shooting the messenger," Chet said.

"I don't know," Jamal said. "There haven't really been a lot of accidents in this race—certainly no more than other adventure races I've seen. And I don't see why anyone would blame Frank and Joe for anything anyway."

"We were a little tough on Frid last night," Frank confessed.

"Long days and frayed nerves got the better of us," Joe added. "We need to stay out of the limelight from now on if we can."

"That'll be difficult if you're going to win the race," Jamal replied.

The Hardys and Chet laughed. The brothers and their friends looked the bikes over and then reviewed the condition of their other gear. Despite the incident the night before, they found no evidence of tampering with their equipment.

Joe shook his head. "I don't get it," he said. "Sabotaging the race seems pretty extreme. And why do it? Could anyone be that desperate to win this race?"

"The prize isn't that big," Frank agreed, "though the exposure could help a career—or a cause."

"What other motive besides wanting to win could there be for sabotaging Speed Times Five?" Chet asked.

"I don't know," Jamal said. "But speaking of exposure, here comes Bennett."

The rugged race organizer looked tired and somewhat rumpled this morning, as opposed to his usual media-ready self. "I want to thank you both for your help after the landslide and for reporting last night's tampering to me," he said. "You're doing a good job—exactly the kind of racers we want in Speed Times Five."

"Some of the other racers don't seem to think so," Chet said.

"Don't worry about them," Bennett replied. "Just

keep doing what you're doing. I've beefed up security, but we couldn't find any trace of the saboteur you said you saw. Neither the sponsors nor I want anything to go wrong with the race. Everyone's going to be extra careful from now on."

"We'll keep our eyes peeled anyway," Joe said.

Bennett nodded and smiled. "I appreciate that. You guys are first class. Good luck in today's stage." He left the group and went to speak to Collins and the other college students.

Today's leg took the competitors on paved roads from St. Esprit to Montreal. Once there, the racers would stay in a hotel before completing the road race and then racing to the finish line in Sea-Zooms—one-person watercraft with high-powered engines that were like motorcycles on water.

Following the race's rules, the teams had converted the bikes used in the cross-country stage for street competition. The bikes' thick mountain tires had been switched to sleek thin ones. The handlebars had been replaced with curved racing grips as well.

The field of competitors had thinned again, both from people dropping out and from planned cutoffs for racers who didn't meet time requirements at each stage. Staggered starts were again the rule of the day, but the open nature of the road race would make it somewhat easier for those in back to catch up with the leaders.

The Hardys found themselves in the middle of the pack, behind Clemenceau, Hawk, and Lupin, but ahead of the college students and Baldwin. The competitors could stop for rest breaks, but doing so too often would harm their chances. Most had water and food packets strapped to the frames of their bikes.

Media coverage was heavy this morning. The entire route would be through streets easily accessible to camera crews. Georges Clemenceau's accident, the landslide, and other incidents had piqued the curiosity of the media. Bennett's staff had a hard time keeping the news cameras out of the way of the race and production crew.

The race began as scheduled, shortly before ten. One side of the road had been blocked off for the race, and the competitors quickly left the campground behind and joined the open highway.

Kelly Hawk broke out early and caught up with Victoria Clemenceau and the lead group just as the Hardys hit the road. Despite the longer than normal rest, the brothers were still stiff from the previous stages of the race.

"I'm using muscles I didn't even know I had," Joe said as he and Frank rode side by side down the road.

"Just think how buff we'll be when we get home," Frank replied. He grabbed the water bottle from his bike frame and squirted a drink into his mouth.

The brothers pedaled as fast as they could while still maintaining a good pace for the whole distance they needed to cover. Soon they drew within striking distance of the lead group.

The pack behind the Hardys had been working hard, too. Some competitors had fallen off the pace, but Baldwin, Curtis, Frid, and Collins were closing in on the leaders as well.

The day wore on, and the smaller groups of racers consolidated into larger ones. By early afternoon the Hardys, Baldwin, and the college students had caught up with the pack containing Clemenceau, Hawk, and Lupin.

The buildings of Montreal rose up in the distance. With their goal in sight, the bikers pushed harder. Clemenceau made a break and moved toward the front of the racers. Lupin went with her, though he didn't look nearly as fresh as the red-clad Canadian racer.

As Clemenceau broke away, the media chase cars followed in the right-hand lane. The camera trucks were careful not to interfere with the other racers. On the left, a sturdy mesh barrier separated the bicyclers from the normal flow of traffic on the road.

A small hill slowed the leaders down and brought them back toward the rest of the pack. The Hardys, Kelly Hawk, and several other racers pushed hard and gained on Lupin and Clemenceau.

Then something went wrong.

It was hard to tell who started it, but the pack in front of Joe and Frank suddenly veered into one another. Bikers brushed knees and shoulders; wheels and hubs collided.

For a moment it looked as if all of the leaders might go down.

Victoria Clemenceau broke out of the pack on the left-hand side, but she seemed to be tangled with Michael Lupin somehow. Her bike wobbled unsteadily—something seemed wrong with the wheels—and she fought to regain control.

Then her tires skidded out from under her and she toppled toward the mesh barrier and the speeding traffic beyond.

10 City Life

Frank and Joe streaked after Victoria as she skidded toward the barrier. As Clemenceau slowed down, Joe caught up with her on the right, while Frank sped in from behind.

Joe reached out with his left hand and grabbed the fabric of Victoria's racing number. At the same time, Frank cut farther to the left, trying to put his bike between her and the oncoming traffic.

He partially succeeded, and Clemenceau's back wheel brushed the front wheel of Frank's bike. The momentary contact kept her from falling and caused her to veer back toward Joe.

"Look out!" she cried, but it was too late for all of them. Bikes and riders slammed into one another. Victoria came out the worst, skidding and falling behind the brothers. She hit the pavement hard, and her helmet bounced off the blacktop.

"Can't control it!" Frank called as he went down, too. A moment later, Joe toppled as well.

The brothers skidded and spun but managed to control their falls better than Clemenceau. Neither one hit his head.

Dazed, the Hardys got up off the pavement as the other racers gave them a wide berth.

"Are you all right?" Joe asked.

"More bruises—a couple of scrapes," Frank replied. "How's Ms. Clemenceau?"

Victoria Clemenceau lay sprawled on the pavement, her bike a twisted mass beside her. She wasn't moving.

Frank and Joe sprinted the short distance between them. Victoria was scraped and bloody, but she was breathing. The Hardys did what they could to administer first aid—immobilizing her head and neck and binding a few of her superficial wounds with bandages from her first-aid kit.

The paramedics arrived almost immediately, each in a powder blue LaTelle Medical & Pharmaceutical outfit. They took over ministering to Clemenceau and checked the Hardys' injuries.

"We're fine, really," Frank said.

"We just want to get back into the race," Joe added.

The lead paramedic nodded. "Well, okay," she said. "If you think you're up to it."

"Hey," Joe replied, "we didn't come all this way just to drop out."

"Well, thanks for the assist," the paramedic said as the brothers returned to their bikes.

"The bikes are pretty banged up, but I think we can keep going—at least until tonight's pit stop," Joe said.

"Yeah," Frank said, twisting his handlebars so they were aligned with his front wheel again. Joe's chain had come untracked, but the two of them quickly got it back together.

By the time the last of the Speed Times Five stragglers passed the scene of the accident, the brothers were back in the race once more.

The accident seemed to have sobered the contestants, and many of the racers were being extra cautious. Still, the Hardys had lost a lot of time. This, and the damage to their bikes, kept them from catching up with the front of the pack.

As the sun set behind them, the brothers wheeled into Montreal. They'd passed a third of the racers, but were still a long way from the leaders.

Their overnight rest stop was at the Hotel d'Etienne, a refurbished building near the old Expo '67 fairgrounds. Just after dusk the brothers checked in with the race officials outside the hotel. They then took their bikes into the underground parking facility, which had been appropriated by the Speed Times Five team.

"Good thing we've got our crew on this stop," Joe said as they walked their battered bikes down the ramp into the garage.

"Yeah, the bikes will need a lot of work if we want to move up in the standings," Frank said.

Near the parking level they ran into Michael Lupin heading the other way.

"Look what the cat dragged in!" Lupin said. "I thought you guys would have packed it in by now."

"We're gluttons for punishment," Joe replied. He and Frank walked past Lupin without looking back.

"You could drop out, you know," Lupin called after them. "No one expects you to win here."

"We'll see you at the finish line, Lupin," Frank shot back.

As the brothers entered the underground facility, Chet and Jamal ran up to them.

"Was Lupin hassling you?" Chet asked.

"Nothing we can't handle," Joe said. Many of the other racers and their support crews looked up as the brothers came in. Joe noted a flash of hostility in several pairs of eyes. "Is there some kind of trouble down here?" he asked.

Jamal shook his head. "Nothing to worry about," he said.

"Some of the racers were wondering why you guys always seem to be nearby when trouble happens," Chet added.

"I hope you set them straight," Frank said.

"Sure," Jamal replied. "We told them you guys are trouble magnets." He smiled to show he was kidding and took Joe's bike. "You have been kind of rough on the equipment, though."

"No rougher than the equipment's been on us," Frank said, handing his bike to Chet.

"Well, don't you two worry about anything," Chet said. "Jamal and I will get the bikes back in shape for tomorrow's leg. You head up to the hotel room and rest. We'll take care of everything."

"Does that include figuring out what the mystery is behind the troubles in this race?" Joe asked.

Chet grinned. "Nope. We'll leave the heavy thinking to you Hardys." He parked Frank's bike in the area designated for their team and hauled out his tool and repair kit.

Jamal parked Joe's bike and both he and Chet began to work. "Are you really sure," Jamal asked as he adjusted Joe's handlebars, "that something mysterious is going on here?"

"Well," Joe replied, "we've had problems with a ski lift. Then my brakes were sabotaged. Someone nearly drowned in the river. Georges Clemenceau got KO'd on the hike. Frank and I nearly got buried by a landslide. And now Victoria Clemenceau almost takes a header into traffic."

"Aside from Joe's brakes, that guy at the bikes last night, and maybe Georges Clemenceau, it could all be coincidence and accidents," Jamal said.

"The news reports say that Victoria's bike had some broken spokes," Chet added, "though that could have happened when she crashed."

"Or it could be what the saboteur was up to last night," Joe said.

"Joe's brakes, Georges's 'accident,' and last night are enough to convince me that someone is messing with the race on purpose," Frank said. "The race competitors seem the most likely suspects."

"But who would want to win that badly?" Chet asked.

"Michael Lupin, Kelly Hawk, and Roger Baldwin could fit that bill," Joe said. "They're the most competitive racers in the pack."

"During the river accident, Lupin shot right by," Jamal noted. "Even Baldwin stopped to help on that one."

"No one's going to nominate Lupin for a humanitarian award, that's for sure," Joe said. "But that doesn't prove he's behind the trouble."

"You heard Hawk's crew talking about sabotage," Chet said. "Her crew isn't very sociable. Maybe they *are* up to something."

"Hawk knows we heard them, though," Frank said. "She and her crew would be stupid to try anything."

"Maybe that's why they've taken to wearing masks," Jamal suggested. "Don't worry about it now, though. Get some rest."

Frank and Joe nodded and headed to the elevator. They had picked up their room assignment and keys when they'd checked in with the race officials, and it was only a short ride to their third-floor room.

"A bit cramped," Frank said, eyeing the two beds, rollaway couch, and cot set up in the room.

"I guess we should have sprung for the deluxe accommodations," Joe remarked, peering out the window leading onto the fire escape. "We've got a lovely view of an alley and the hotel's service entrance, though."

"Open the window, would you?" Frank asked. "I could use some air."

"You've been sucking wind all day," Joe said, grinning as he opened the window.

"I'm just tired of eating your dust," Frank joked.

They both showered and changed and then collapsed onto their beds.

"Man, does this feel good after a couple nights in the woods!" Joe said.

"Don't get too comfortable," Frank replied. "We've got a long push to the finish tomorrow."

"And an early-morning wake-up call," Joe added with a sigh. Both of them lay on their backs for a couple of minutes, staring up at the ceiling.

Finally, Frank asked, "What did you say?"

Joe shook his head. "I didn't say anything," he replied.

Frank sat up and looked toward the window.

"What is it?" Joe asked.

"Someone is talking outside," Frank whispered. "Something about the race." He and Joe rose from their beds and tiptoed to the window. Because of the fire escape, they had to lean out a bit to improve their view.

99

Two men stood in the shadows of the alley below, talking. Both were dressed in dark outfits: one in a business suit, the other in jogging clothes. The shadows made it impossible for the brothers to recognize either of them. The men spoke in hushed tones, but the Hardys could make out some of the words.

". . . according to plan," the man in jogging clothes said.

"Good," said the man in the suit. "I wouldn't want any problems at this late stage."

"There won't be any," the other man replied. "You didn't even need to come here tonight."

"I like to check on my operatives personally," the man in the suit said. "We've got a lot riding on this race."

The man in the jogging outfit chuckled. "Don't worry, with me and the 'crew' you provided on the job, this is one race I guarantee will turn out as planned," he said. "I'll see you after the big finish."

The man in the suit nodded and headed down the alley toward the street. The other man turned as though he might enter the hotel's back door, but then he paused. He turned and began walking down the alley in the opposite direction from the other man. As he did so, he pulled the hood of his jogging outfit up over his head.

"He must have spotted us!" Joe whispered.

"Too late now," Frank said. "But if we use the fire escape, we might still be able to catch them."

The brothers opened the window and ducked

onto the wrought-iron fire escape outside. They scampered down the steps and dropped into the alley just in time to see the dapper man get into a long black limo and speed away.

Frank peered after the car. "I can almost make out the plate number. It's MP . . . zero one . . . or . . . Rats! It's just too dark."

"We might still catch the other guy," Joe said, looking from the vanishing car to the man walking quickly in the other direction.

They sprinted down the alley just as the man in the hood turned left, heading away from the hotel. By the time they got to the sidewalk, he was already on the other side of the street, walking away very quickly.

The Hardys turned the corner and ran after him.

The man glanced back slightly and increased his pace, keeping ahead of the brothers. As he ran, he pulled a cell phone out of his pocket and began speaking into it.

"Who do you think he's calling?" Joe asked.

Frank shrugged. "A cab, maybe?"

The man turned around another bend and disappeared from view. When the Hardys rounded the corner moments later, the man was nowhere in sight. Commercial buildings lined the deserted street and there was a Montreal subway stop at the end of the block.

"The metro?" Frank asked.

"Must be," Joe concluded, running to the subway entrance. A long stairway descended from a landing just inside the door. They caught a glimpse of their quarry moving away at the bottom of the stairs before he disappeared onto the metro platform.

Tossing some Canadian bills from their pockets to the ticket taker for fare, the brothers flew down the stairway after the hooded man.

Rush hour had long passed, and the station was nearly deserted. A train stood waiting at the platform, but the brothers saw no sign of their quarry.

"He must have boarded the train," Joe said. "The only exit is the way we came."

"Hop on," Frank said. "The train's leaving."

He and Joe darted into the nearest train car just as the doors slid closed. A look into the only car behind them indicated the hooded man must be farther forward.

The Hardys ducked through the compartment's front door as the train pulled out of the station. They moved from compartment to compartment as the train zipped through the Montreal underground. A few people sat quietly in some of the cars, but the brothers saw no sign of the hooded man. At each stop, the Hardys checked to make sure their quarry didn't get off. Then they resumed the search.

"He must be moving forward, same as we are," Frank said.

"Well, he's going to run out of cars soon," Joe replied.

Frank's hypothesis proved correct. As they

entered the second car from the engine, they saw their target in the frontmost car. The man stood by the farthest exit door, still talking on his phone.

"We've got him now," Joe said as they ran through the intervening car. They opened the last door just as the train pulled into a new station. As the metro slowed to a stop, the hooded man exited to the platform, pushing past several men boarding the train.

"C'mon," Joe said, sprinting for the exit. But as he did, two of the new passengers stepped in front of the door.

"Where do you think you're going?" one of the men growled.

11 Metro Mania

The men barring the brothers' way were large, as large as the biggest member of Kelly Hawk's crew. They were dressed in jeans and sweatshirts with the hoods pulled up over their heads. The Hardys could see the men's faces, and though they looked vaguely familiar, neither brother could place them.

"We're getting off the train," Frank said.

"Not at this station," the man in the powder blue sweatshirt said. "Not the way me and Pierre see it. Right, Pierre?"

Pierre, wearing a black sweatshirt, nodded. "Right, Jacques," he said.

Frank tried to push past the men, but Jacques put out one beefy arm and stopped him. "You don't wanna do that," Jacques said.

"Why not just wait," Pierre suggested. "Get off at the next station—no hard feelings."

"The only hard feeling you'll get is my fist on your nose if you don't move," Joe said.

Pierre and Jacques glanced at each other. "You mean, like this?" Pierre said, swinging for Joe's head.

Joe ducked out of the way and slammed his fist into Pierre's abs. The big man grunted but didn't move. He smiled at Joe as the younger Hardy shook his fist. "The guy's made of rocks!" Joe said.

But Frank wasn't listening. He was too busy trying to avoid Jacques, who had lowered his head and charged the older Hardy. Frank tried to step aside, but Jacques wrapped his arms around Frank's waist and carried him backward.

As the doors to the car slid closed, the only other passenger slipped back out onto the platform, leaving the Hardys alone with the thugs.

Pierre threw another punch at Joe, but the younger Hardy danced back. Frank brought his knee up into Jacques's stomach as the two of them hit the floor. The air rushed out of Jacques's lungs and Frank rolled away from him.

The elder Hardy regained his feet and aimed a martial arts kick at Jacques's head. Jacques brought up his arm and partially blocked the blow. He staggered back, his face glowing red with anger. "Now you have made me angry!" he said.

Frank and Joe took up defensive positions in the middle of the car, standing next to each other.

Jacques charged again, with Pierre coming in behind him.

The brothers parted in the middle as the big men bore in. Frank stepped aside and threw a spin kick at the back of Jacques's head. Joe ducked under another punch and slammed his foot into Pierre's knee.

The thugs grunted and collapsed onto the row of seats just beyond the Hardys. Before the brothers could press their advantage, though, the big men spun and lunged to their feet.

Jacques's shoulder caught Frank in the stomach. The air rushed out of the elder Hardy's lungs as his back smashed into the wall of the metro car.

Joe ducked under another punch, but Pierre followed up with a quick knee that caught Joe in the ribs. Joe crashed to the floor. He grabbed a seat and pulled himself up once again just as Pierre threw a vicious kick at his head.

His head spinning, Frank karate-chopped both sides of Jacques's neck. The hooded thug howled in pain and backed away. Frank leaped forward and grabbed the vertical handrail in the center of the compartment. Using his momentum, the elder Hardy spun around the pole and kicked Jacques full in the chest with both feet. Jacques flew through the air and slammed into the door leading to the adjoining car.

Joe dodged to the side and Pierre's kick brushed by his shoulder. The younger Hardy countered with a swift right cross. He caught Pierre square on the jaw and the thug toppled backward, landing only a few feet from Jacques.

Dazed, the big men staggered to their feet as the Hardys came at them again. With only a slight glance at each other for confirmation, the thugs opened the door into the next compartment and darted through it.

The Hardys charged the door, but Pierre held the door handle tight while Jacques opened the door on the far side of the car. As the brothers finally yanked the door open, Pierre sprinted for the opposite door. The Hardys and the thug dashed past a few startled passengers, each trying to reach the far door first. Jacques called encouragement to his compatriot while the bystanders in the car cowered out of the way.

Just as it seemed the brothers would pull the trailing thug down, Pierre grabbed a frightened old lady from her seat and thrust her at the Hardys. Frank and Joe stopped, making sure the old woman didn't fall or hurt herself. But as they did that, Pierre and Jacques darted into the next car and pulled the door shut.

They grabbed an umbrella from a passenger and jammed it in the door handles, just as the Hardys reached the door. Before the brothers could break through, the train pulled into the metro station at Lionel-Groulx.

"They're getting out!" Joe said, seeing Pierre and Jacques dash onto the station platform. He and Frank bolted out as the train doors slid shut once more.

The station at Lionel-Groulx was a modern, multilevel complex, with tall ceilings and balcony walkways. The thugs sprinted up the escalator from the platforms to the first balcony, pushing surprised riders aside as they went.

The Hardys dashed after them, though the brothers were careful not to harm any of the riders they passed. "A guy could get killed falling from these escalators," Joe noted as they topped the first escalator.

"Or the balconies," Frank added. "Duck!" As he spoke, a big trash can, thrown by Pierre, sailed over his head.

But Joe didn't hear the warning in time. The heavy container hit him in the chest, and he toppled backward into the balcony railing. For a moment it looked as though he might go over. Then Frank grabbed the front of his brother's shirt and hauled him back to the floor as the thugs dashed down a stairway on the other side of the balcony.

"Phew!" Joe said. "Thanks for the save."

Frank nodded. "Don't mention it. The bad guys are getting away."

He and Joe ran to the stairs the thugs had taken and started down it. As they did so, Pierre and Jacques boarded a train at the platform. The metro's doors slid closed behind the thugs before the Hardys could reach the platform. As the brothers watched in frustration, the train left the station.

Joe slapped his fist onto the concrete stair railing. "Man!" he said. "I wanted to catch those guys!"

"They knew this station better than we did," Frank said. "They lured us here on purpose. We didn't stand much of a chance."

"If I ever see them again, though . . ." Joe said.

"Let's get back to the hotel," Frank said. "Jamal and Chet must be wondering where we are."

Chet and Jamal had plenty of questions for the brothers when the Hardys got back to their room. Frank filled their friends in while Joe brought Vince Bennett up to date. When they'd finished, Chet asked, "And you have no idea who this hooded man is?"

"We're thinking he must be one of the competitors," Frank said, "or part of someone's crew. Whoever he is, clearly he's up to no good."

"But if he's part of the race, why didn't he just go back into the hotel to get away from you?" Jamal asked.

"He knew we'd spotted him," Joe replied, "so he tried to throw us off the scent. And his buddies nearly threw me off a metro balcony."

"Why, though?" Chet said. "Just to win the race?"

"Could be," Frank said. "The guy in the suit said there was a lot riding on the race."

"I get the feeling we're still missing part of this picture, though," Joe said.

"Maybe it'll be clearer once we've slept on it," Jamal suggested. "After all, we've got an early start tomorrow."

Joe groaned. "And I thought this was going to be the evening to rest and recover!"

On the last day of the race, the brothers and their friends woke before sunrise. Joe and Frank felt tired and beat up, and a quick breakfast made them feel only a little better. After eating, they all went down to the garage to check the bikes. Most of the other competitors and their crews were there as well.

Lupin and his hired help shot a suspicious glare at the brothers as they entered the underground lot. Maggie Collins waved a weak hello, for which Quentin Curtis and Robert Frid scowled at her. Roger Baldwin ignored the brothers entirely, as did John and Jim from Kelly Hawk's crew. Kelly, though, walked over to the Hardys' work area as the four friends gave their bikes a final once-over.

"See, boys?" she said. "You don't have to hold a minority political view to get folks suspicious. Sometimes all you have to do is to be in the wrong place at the wrong time." A sly grin tugged at the edges of her mouth.

Joe and Frank chuckled. "Good luck today, Kelly," Frank said.

"Yeah, see you at the finish line," Joe added.

"You guys, too," she replied. "And keep your noses clean." She went back to her preparation area and huddled with her crew.

Vince Bennett came by to wish all the remaining racers good luck. Once again he privately thanked the Hardys for keeping their eyes open, though he had nothing to report on the hooded man.

Because they had helped Victoria Clemenceau the previous day, the Hardys were still far back in the pack when the race started again. Still, the road portion from Montreal to St. Jean-sur-Richelieu gave them a good chance to make up some ground.

The remaining bike portion of the race passed uneventfully and the brothers pulled into the waterside checkpoint well before noon—back in the hunt once more. Dozens of SeaZoom personal watercraft lined the beach outside of town, waiting for the final leg of the Speed Times Five Adventure Race.

Support crews worked feverishly, preparing the crafts so the small jetboats would be ready when their drivers' turn to start came. Michael Lupin, Roger Baldwin, and Kelly Hawk were among the leaders, as Vince Bennett prepared to start the mad dash for the finish line in Burlington, Vermont.

"It'll be good to get back in the USA," Jamal said.

"Just make sure you're ready to meet us for the trophy ceremony," Joe said with a smile.

"We'll be there," Chet replied, "unless Jamal's driving gets us in trouble with the border patrol."

They all laughed.

As the Hardys and their friends completed their final checks and stashed equipment, food, and water in the storage compartments under the SeaZooms' seats, the race leaders were finishing the final paperwork before starting.

Baldwin, Hawk, Lupin, and three others gave a last smile to the cameras before taking their positions. As they did, Frank spotted someone familiar walking away from Roger Baldwin's SeaZoom.

"Pierre!" Frank gasped.

"Where?" asked Joe.

"Near Baldwin's SeaZoom," Frank said. "In the blue paramedic uniform and hat. I almost didn't recognize him."

He and Joe rose to their feet and started to dash toward the starting area.

"We'll never make it!" Joe said as they ran.

With a final glance to the stands, Baldwin hopped on his jetboat and revved it up. At a signal from the starter, he gunned the engine and zoomed out into the waterway, heading toward Lake Champlain.

"Wait! Stop the race!" Frank called.

It was too late, though. Just a hundred yards offshore, Baldwin's SeaZoom veered suddenly to the right. The brothers watched in horror as Baldwin headed straight for the metal pylons of an old wharf.

12 The Black Boat

Baldwin struggled with the control column of the SeaZoom but to no avail. At the last second, he bailed out of the jetboat as it smashed into the rusting pylons. The SeaZoom exploded into pieces, raining fragments everywhere. People ran for cover as the shrapnel fell on the water and near the frightened spectators on the old dock.

"Where's Baldwin?" Joe said as emergency crews raced toward the scene of the crash.

"I don't see him," Frank said, scanning the surface of the water.

As he spoke, though, Baldwin's helmeted head popped up. He floundered a bit as the rescue boats came nearer. Several rescue divers jumped in next to him and soon they were dragging Baldwin into their boat.

Half frantic, Vince Bennett ran toward the staging beach. "Clear the way!" he said. "Make room for the rescue boat! We need to keep the race going, too!"

As he passed by the Hardys, Frank stopped him and said, "Why not just restart the leg?"

"We've already got racers in the water," Bennett said. "It wouldn't be fair to call them back, not when we've got a chance to keep things going. Every race has accidents."

"This race has had more than its share, though," Frank said. "I saw someone near Bennett's Sea-Zoom before he started—one of the guys Joe and I had a run-in with last night: Pierre."

"He was pretending to be part of the medical crew," Joe added. "Which is why he seemed familiar when we ran into him in the subway."

"Maybe they've been working the race, causing trouble all along," Frank suggested.

Bennett frowned, glancing from the brothers to where the rescue team was docking with Baldwin. The former triathlete seemed to be waving away all attempts to help him. Bennett walked in that direction, and the Hardys tagged along.

"Did you actually see this Pierre try to sabotage the race?" Bennett asked.

"Well, no, but . . . ," Joe said.

"Look, guys," Bennett said, stopping just short of the rescue boat, "the sponsors would kill me if I stopped the race now. Talk to my security chief about the man you saw. I don't know what we can do about him, though, even if he was involved with this accident." He turned to Baldwin. "Hey, Roger, are you all right?"

"All right?" Baldwin snarled as he pulled off his helmet. "I'm bruised and wet and out of the race. How would you be?"

Bennett looked sheepish. "I'm sure the press would like a word or two with you," he said. "If you feel up to it before the medics check you over."

Baldwin hopped out of the rescue boat. He was bruised and scraped, but didn't look much the worse for wear. He let out a long, angry sigh. "Sure," he said, "I'll say a few words before I head home."

"I'll get you to the EMTs right after," Bennett said.

"I can find my own way to the medics," Baldwin countered. "Let's just get this over with."

Bennett put his arm around the dejected racer's shoulders. "That's the spirit," Bennett said. Together, the two of them walked toward the group of reporters. As they got there, Bennett turned to one of his staff members and said, "Keep the race going."

Joe fumed. "I can't believe he's not even going to investigate this," he said.

"Business is business," Jamal said. He and Chet had caught up with the Hardys as the brothers were speaking to the race organizer.

"Let's talk to the security chief and get back to our boats," Frank said.

"Yeah," Chet urged. "Your start times are coming up quickly." As he spoke, the starters launched another competitor's boat into the water.

"Get the final prep done," Joe said to Chet and Jamal. "Frank and I will be there in a few minutes."

It frustrated Joe that the security chief spent so little time talking to them. Still, Frank pointed out that the man obviously had a lot to keep track of with the start of the last leg under way.

"He said he'd check with the LMP medical crew," Frank noted. "We really couldn't ask for more with so much going on. Our best bet is to get back to the competition and keep our eyes open."

Joe nodded and the two of them rejoined their crew near the beach staging area. As they arrived, Baldwin left in one of the LaTelle Medical & Pharmaceutical vans. The ambulance pulled away quickly, its siren blaring.

"Boy, I hope he didn't have a delayed reaction to the crash," Joe said.

"They're probably just being cautious," Frank added.

The atmosphere at the starting line was one of controlled frenzy. Race officials scurried everywhere, making last-minute preparations as the lead competitors launched in rapid succession.

Michael Lupin started shortly after the Baldwin crash, and Kelly Hawk zoomed off the line a few racers later. More competitors hit the water, and the Hardys' start time approached quickly. Just ahead of them, Curtis, Collins, and Frid churned up the placid waterway.

"You guys still have a chance to win," Jamal said to the brothers, "but you'll have to make up a lot of time."

"So no detours along the way," Chet cautioned.

"We'll keep our noses clean," Joe said with a smile.

"Which should be easy, since we're racing in the water," Frank added with a chuckle.

When their numbers were called, the Hardys and their friends quickly carried their SeaZooms to the water's edge and made their final checks. The race had gone smoothly since Baldwin's rough start, and even Bennett was smiling once more. The TV crews seemed thrilled with the excitement of the competition. Helicopters buzzed in the distance, tracking the leaders.

As the starter yelled, "Go!" Joe, Chet, and Jamal pushed the younger Hardy's sleek jetboat into the water. Joe hit the throttle and zoomed out into the cold, clear channel. Frank pulled on his racing helmet. Less than a minute later, Chet and Jamal launched Frank's boat as well.

The elder Hardy quickly caught up with his brother, and the two of them kept pace as they zipped across the water.

The day was cool and sunny, with just a hint of a breeze churning up the surface of the raceway. The noise of the SeaZoom engines was loud in the brothers' ears, making normal conversation difficult. Still, they could hear the engines of the competitors in front of them, and the buzz of the pack trailing behind.

Chet had stowed a pair of waterproof walkie-talkies in with the brothers' gear, and Frank hauled his out as they zipped along. He motioned to Joe, and the younger Hardy did the same.

"I think I see Hawk and Lupin up ahead, past those channel islands," Frank said.

"They're making good time," Joe said. "We'll have a tough job catching up to them. The college kids are a lot closer, though. We might be able to pass them by the time we hit the border."

The late morning was perfect for water racing, and as the sun arced past noon, the air warmed as well.

The brothers' sleek craft bounded over the waves, spraying tiny rainbows into the afternoon sky. The Hardys ate on the fly, pulling prepackaged food from pouches hanging at their belts—under their life jackets—and then stowing the wrappers.

The wind picked up a bit as they crossed the U.S.-Canadian border. The water grew choppy as the brothers passed beneath the bridge near Rouses Point. As the water became rougher, the racers began to bunch up once more.

"The waves are slowing down the pack," Joe said into his walkie-talkie.

Frank nodded. "That gives us a better chance," he said. "But we'll have to drive really well to catch Lupin and Hawk."

"Yeah," Joe replied. "They've got a good lead. I can only see them when we've got a straight, clear stretch of water."

"With the wind coming from the east, they're using the central islands as a wind break," Frank added. "That makes them harder to see and also lets them drive in smoother water."

Joe smiled. "Sounds like you think we should adopt that strategy, too," he said.

"Well," Frank said, "do you want to win or not?"

In response, Joe gunned the throttle and surged ahead of his older brother once more. Frank leaned forward over his sleek craft and zipped after Joe.

By carefully plotting their course between the islands and the open water, the brothers made up even more ground. They'd closed on Frid, Collins, Curtis, and the middle of the field and—as the group passed Isle La Motte—came within striking distance of the front of the pack.

Swirling waves had slowed Lupin, Hawk, and the leaders further, despite their clever island-hugging strategy. Hawk and Lupin jockeyed for the lead, weaving back and forth just enough to fend off other competitors.

"They're lucky that the Clemenceaus and Baldwin are out of the race," Joe said. "Very lucky."

"A motive for sabotage, you're thinking?" Frank replied.

Joe shrugged as he bounced over the chilly water. "We haven't come up with a better motive than wanting to win," he said. "And we know that Hawk's crew was thinking of putting the kibosh on other racers."

"I was beginning to think it was Baldwin," Frank said. "He always seemed to be around the 'accidents,' even when he wasn't involved. Remember when we passed him in the woods without seeing him? He could have KO'd Georges during that time and pulled his body off the trail."

"He's certainly strong enough to overpower someone," Joe said, "and fast enough to keep pace with runners like you and me. But now that he's in the hospital . . . ," He shrugged. "I keep thinking that there's some vital clue we're overlooking."

"This case would be easier to solve if we weren't trying to run a race at the same time," Frank said with a sigh.

Occasional helicopters buzzed overhead as they raced down the lake past the wooded shores of Grand Isle. Most were observation craft, covering the race for TV stations. A few, though, were tourists, just wanting a first-hand look at the contest.

Spectators occasionally dotted the lakeshore as well, and private boats sometimes trailed the fast-moving racers for a while.

The pack dipped and swooped around the small islets dotting the edge of Grand Isle, each racer looking for the best water—the best conditions to outrun the other competitors.

A racer near the front of the group hit a submerged log and tumbled into the cold water. She popped to the surface immediately and waved for the trailing rescue crews.

Her accident, though, forced Lupin and Hawk to veer out of the way and cost them both precious time. The rest of the pack took advantage of the mishap and nearly caught the leaders.

Frank glanced back as the rescue boat picked up the floundering racer.

"A normal accident, you think?" Joe asked.

"At this point, who can tell?" Frank replied, frustration showing through in his voice. "Let's just catch the leaders."

He throttled up and zoomed through the pack toward Hawk and Lupin. Joe followed in his wake, angling for the smooth water to save time and fuel.

They passed between Maggie Collins and Robert Frid, neither of whom was taking the best tack. Quentin Curtis was hugging closer to the islands than the rest and remained slightly in front of the brothers, though behind Lupin and Hawk.

As the Hardys set their sights on the leaders, something to the east caught their eye. A huge black SeaZoom burst into the lake from behind one of the small barrier islands.

"Another spectator, maybe?" Joe asked.

"If he is, he's coming in awfully fast," Frank said. "Doesn't he know the race has the right of way?"

If the driver of the black jetboat knew, he didn't care. Rather than veering off as he neared the racers, he drove straight toward the pack.

13 Shipwrecked

"Look out!" Joe cried as the black SeaZoom swooped toward them.

At the last second, though, the intruder turned and fell into pace with the rest of the pack.

"Who does he think he is?" Joe asked.

The other racers had spotted the intruder as well and cast nervous glances at the black-helmeted rider in their midst.

The black jetboat was larger and faster than the one-person SeaZooms the competitors were riding. It paced the group easily as its driver checked out the individual racers.

"I think he's looking for something," Frank said.

No sooner had Frank spoken than the black-garbed racer zoomed ahead of the Hardys and to the left, toward the small islands.

"He's heading for Quentin Curtis!" Joe said.

The black SeaZoom rocketed toward where the college student was navigating the smooth waters closer to the shore. The intruder cut in front of Curtis, forcing the racer to veer sharply.

Curtis turned toward the islands to get out of the new racer's way. The black craft dogged him, forcing him farther into the shallows. Curtis fumbled for his emergency radio, his wet fingers having trouble getting a grip on the radio's plastic surface.

The black SeaZoom dashed past him on the right. The bigger craft's wake shook Curtis's jetboat, and he lost hold of the emergency phone. It tumbled through the air and landed in the lake.

Curtis tried to turn back toward the rest of the field, but the black boat cut him off once more. Even as the two moved down the lake, the intruder was slowly but surely forcing Quentin Curtis toward the rocky shoreline.

Seeing their friend's predicament, Maggie Collins and Robert Frid left the pack and angled toward Curtis and the intruder.

"I don't know what's going on here," Frank said into his walkie-talkie, "but I think we should put a stop to it."

Joe nodded. "We're closer than Curtis's friends," he said. "It means giving up any chance of winning the race, though."

Frank paused for only a moment. "If that's the way it's got to be . . . ," he said. He angled his boat for the shoals and turned the throttle up all the way.

Side by side the Hardys shot over the water, heading toward Curtis and the black SeaZoom. Collins and Frid trailed behind them, but they were neither as close to Curtis nor as skilled in their boats as the brothers.

The black racer seemed to notice the pursuit and pressed his harassment of Curtis. He cut closer and closer to the harried student, barely missing colliding with the smaller SeaZoom. Curtis maneuvered his boat frantically, trying to avoid the rocky shoals, and the larger craft circling him.

Curtis dodged, then wove, then nearly floundered. He turned too sharply and water washed over the back of his SeaZoom. The black racer darted past, reached out with one hand, and yanked Curtis from the saddle.

The college student sailed through the air for several feet before crashing face first into the water. The intruder swung back around and threw a rope around the smaller craft. Then he gunned the engine and headed for a channel between the small islands along the coast with Curtis's SeaZoom in tow.

Curtis bobbed to the surface, his head and neck supported by his life preserver.

"What is going on here?" Joe asked.

Frank shrugged. "It seems like a lot of trouble to steal a SeaZoom," he said. "We'd better get to Curtis. Even with that life vest he might still drown if he's unconscious."

Curtis swayed gently in the waves as the brothers came to his rescue.

"He's out cold, all right," Joe said. "Get on the horn and get the rescue team in here." He pulled near the unconscious racer and hopped off his Sea-Zoom.

"Check," Frank said, holstering his walkie-talkie and taking out the emergency radio.

Using rescue swimming techniques, Joe quickly towed Curtis alongside Frank's watercraft. "I don't think he's hurt badly," Joe said. "The water's pretty chilly, though."

"The medics are on their way," Frank said. "And here come Curtis's friends, too."

Maggie Collins and Robert Frid skidded over the waves toward the Hardys and the unconscious student. The Hardys saw concern in the eyes of the other coeds.

"Is he all right?" Maggie asked, pulling off her helmet.

"We should try to get him out of the water," Joe responded. "It's pretty cold and we don't want him going into shock."

Working together, they lifted Curtis aboard the back of Maggie Collins's SeaZoom. Curtis groaned and coughed. "Don't move him too much before the EMTs arrive," Joe said. "He might have some internal injuries."

Collins cradled her friend's helmeted head on her lap while Frid kept both their boats steady.

"Do you have any idea who might have done this, or why?" Frank asked the students.

Collins and Frid shook their heads. "I can't

imagine," Collins said. "I don't know why anyone would want to hurt Quentin."

Joe climbed back on board his SeaZoom. "Was there some reason someone might have wanted to steal that SeaZoom?" he asked.

Collins and Frid exchanged a nervous glance.

"You don't think he wants the medicine, do you?" Collins asked.

"It couldn't be," Frid said. "The medicine can't be worth *that* much."

"What medicine?" Frank and Joe asked simultaneously.

"A guy back in the States hired us to bring some meds across the border for him," Collins replied. "He said his mother needed them, and the price was too high in the U.S. We were bringing back a whole year's supply."

Frank nodded. "I've heard that the Canadian health-care system sometimes makes prescriptions less expensive than in the U.S."

"Someone delivered the meds to us just before the start of the Speed Times Five competition," Frid said. "We stashed it with our race equipment and took turns carrying it during the race."

"Let me guess," Joe said. "Quentin Curtis was carrying it today."

Robert Frid and Maggie Collins nodded sheepishly. "It was in the storage compartment under his seat—along with his emergency gear."

Frank let out a long, slow breath. "You two take care of your friend. The medics will be here soon,"

Frank said. "Come on, Joe. We've got work to do."

"Are you getting back in the race?" Maggie Collins asked, wiping tears from the corners of her eyes.

"No," Frank said. "We're going after the guy who did this."

He and Joe kicked their SeaZooms back into high gear and sped away on the same course the black SeaZoom had taken.

Joe hauled out his walkie-talkie again. "I guess it didn't occur to the three of them that this was a pretty complex plan just to smuggle prescription medicine," he said.

"Yeah," Frank said. "I think that black racer, whoever he is, has bigger fish to fry."

"Among the racers, Lupin and Hawk were at the top of my list," Joe said. "But they were dueling for the lead, and I doubt either one could have doubled back and changed SeaZooms. It could be Hawk's crew, though, or one of the thugs we ran into before."

"We saw Pierre at the boat launch," Frank said. "Though he could have gotten ahead of us using a car or chopper, I suppose. Or it could be Jacques in that boat."

"We'll know as soon as we catch this perp," Joe replied.

The brothers raced between the small islands and soon caught sight of the rogue SeaZoom once more. Though the intruder's vessel was larger and faster, towing Curtis's boat was slowing it down.

He cut through the strait into Mallett's Bay with the Hardys in hot pursuit. Water sprayed from behind the brothers' SeaZooms and dripped from Joe's racing suit.

"How are you doing, Joe?" Frank asked.

"I've been warmer," Joe said, shivering slightly. "I'll heat things up but good, though, when we catch this joker."

The black boat skirted toward Grand Isle again, trying to put some smaller islets between itself and the brothers. Slowly but surely, though, the Hardys were gaining on him.

Joe glanced at his brother. "It just occurred to me—if this is a smuggling scam, the guy behind it might *not* be causing the race's troubles."

"Or he could have caused them as a distraction," Frank said. "Whoever he is—even if he's a contestant or crew member—winning the race clearly isn't part of his plan."

Joe nodded. "His priority is getting whatever's in that SeaZoom into the U.S. without being spotted by customs agents. Could he be messing the race up to distract attention from himself?"

"That's my guess," Frank said. "Diverting officials' attention would be a high priority—nearly as high as getting the goods across the border."

"Hey!" Joe said. "I just remembered something we heard that didn't seem important at the time. It could be the key to solving this case."

"If it involves a news report and a license plate, I just had the same idea myself," Frank said.

"The question remains, though: Who's in that boat?"

"Only one way to find out," Frank replied, gunning the throttle.

The black SeaZoom darted into the small space between two islets, still heading up the coast toward its unknown destination. As Frank and Joe approached the strait, though, two more black watercraft came storming in the opposite direction—right toward them.

The men driving the new intruder boats weren't wearing helmets. Even from a distance, the Hardys recognized them.

"Jacques and Pierre," Frank said. "I guess that means they're not in the main boat."

"It also means that you were right about someone being able to cut ahead of us in a car or helicopter," Joe said.

A grim smile tugged at the corners of his mouth. "Come on, Frank," he said. "We still owe these goons for the metro."

The thugs charged toward the brothers. Pierre swung a rope over his head as he bore in, while Jacques was carrying a long pole resembling a broom handle.

Pierre skidded in front of the brothers, throwing a huge spray of water in the Hardys' faces. At the same time, he tossed the rope toward Frank.

Blinking the water from his eyes, the older Hardy ducked just in time to avoid being snared by Pierre's lasso.

Jacques swung his pole at Joe's head. The younger Hardy swerved out of the way and started after the black racer once more. When he glanced back to check the pursuit, though, he saw that both thugs were aiming for Frank.

Water flew from Joe's SeaZoom as he circled back to help his brother.

Pierre and Jacques were trying to catch Frank in a pincer movement between their boats. With both the pole and the rope coming at him, Frank didn't seem to have much of a chance.

The older Hardy looked at the thugs and their weapons, trying to gauge whether he'd have to abandon ship to dodge them both. The prospect of the chilly water wasn't too attractive, though it was considerably more appealing than being strangled or clobbered.

His face broke into a grim smile as he saw Joe speeding to his rescue. Hoping to buy a few seconds so Joe could help him out, Frank wheeled his SeaZoom and headed for shore.

The thugs closed in on the older Hardy. With his back toward them, there seemed little chance that Frank could dodge both their attacks.

Pierre threw his rope and Frank ducked. This set him up to be hammered by Jacques's pole—but the blow never came.

As Jacques reeled back to hit the older Hardy, Joe zipped up behind and grabbed the pole. Joe and Jacques tugged furiously for a few moments before Joe finally pulled the weapon out of the thug's grip.

Doing so unbalanced the younger Hardy, though. He lost control of his SeaZoom and fell overboard as his jetboat tumbled into a spectacular crash.

Joe surfaced immediately and shook the water from his eyes. As his vision cleared, he saw Pierre's SeaZoom heading right for him.

14 Duel at Sea

Frank wheeled his SeaZoom around again, just in time to see his brother's predicament—but he was too far away to do anything about it.

As Jacques recovered his balance, Pierre gunned the throttle and drove straight toward Joe. The younger Hardy started to swim for shore, but he had no chance against the powerful SeaZoom.

Frank raced toward Joe, knowing he'd never get there in time.

Pierre leaned over the control column of his Sea-Zoom, making a final correction to ensure that he'd hit Joe full on.

At the last second, Joe dove under the water, kicking for all he was worth.

Pierre passed harmlessly over the younger Hardy's

head. Joe resurfaced a safe distance behind his antagonist just as Frank barreled up to him.

"Hop on!" Frank said, extending his hand. The elder Hardy slowed down his SeaZoom just enough to grab Joe.

Joe scrambled aboard as Pierre and Jacques regrouped and swung their jetboats toward the Hardys once more.

"We can't outrun them with my extra weight," Joe said.

"Then we'll have to outthink them," Frank replied grimly.

As the brothers turned, Pierre and Jacques came up with a new plan. Maneuvering close together, Pierre tossed one end of his rope to his partner. Jacques grabbed hold and the two of them stretched the rope between them like a clothesline. They sped straight toward the brothers, holding the rope at neck height.

Frank gunned the throttle and headed right toward the thugs.

"Frank," Joe said, "I don't think we can get around them, either."

"I know," Frank replied. "So we'll just have to go *through*. When I give the signal, help me skip the SeaZoom into the air."

"You want to go up?"

Frank nodded and a grim smile tugged at his mouth. "Only long enough to get some momentum for going down."

"I get you," Joe said, "but it's pretty risky."

As the villains bore in with their deadly clothes-line, Frank said, "So is racing. Ready? Now!"

He and Joe both rode up on the machine, lifting its nose out of the water momentarily. In the next instant Frank thrust the nose down and the machine dove.

As the line streaked toward them, the SeaZoom crashed down, burying the front of the machine in the chilly water. The rest of the sleek boat followed, taking the Hardys with it. The rope passed harm-lessly over the brothers' heads as the villains whizzed past.

With the air intakes submerged, the engine of the Hardys' jetboat sputtered and nearly died. Then the craft's natural buoyancy brought them back to the surface and the motor roared to life. Frank spun them around toward their attackers.

"That was close!" Joe said.

"I figured if it worked for one of us, it'd work for both of us," Frank replied.

"I'm glad we practiced that trick last summer vacation," Joe said. "Though I never thought we'd use it on a case." He pulled off his helmet and shook the water from his blond hair.

"Why'd you take your helmet off?" Frank asked.

"Get me close to Pierre," Joe said, "and you'll see."

The brothers' stunt had confused the thugs. Jacques and Pierre discovered they couldn't wheel around effectively while holding the rope. Jacques dropped his end, and both villains began to turn back toward the Hardys.

Frank cut his SeaZoom toward Pierre as the thug reeled in his rope and was turning to make another pass at the brothers.

As the Hardys swung in close, Joe threw his helmet at Pierre. The thug ducked, and the motion threw him off balance. As Pierre's SeaZoom slowed, Joe leaped from the back of Frank's watercraft onto the seat behind Pierre.

Pierre turned in his seat but not fast enough. Joe slammed his fist into the thug's midsection. The air rushed out of Pierre's lungs. Joe followed up with a clout to the villain's jaw. Pierre's head flew back, and he sailed off the SeaZoom and splashed down into the chilly water of Lake Champlain. His life vest kept the unconscious villain from sinking.

Joe scrambled forward and took the craft's controls. He jockeyed the machine next to Frank as the other thug barreled toward them.

The next moment, though, the truth of the situation sank into Jacques's mind. Realizing he was now outnumbered, Jacques slowed his watercraft and began to turn.

Frank smiled. "It would have been smarter for them if they'd taken off when your boat got swamped," he said. "They could have outrun us easily, then. Now, though. . . !"

Joe smiled in return. "Let's get him!"

The brothers streaked forward as Jacques turned tail and ran.

"Herd him that way," Joe yelled, pointing.

Frank nodded, and the two of them zipped along either side of the thug, corralling him the way they wanted him to go.

Jacques glanced back as he ran, fear in his eyes. He didn't see Joe's abandoned SeaZoom until it was too late. The watercraft sat half-submerged in the water, just where it had been when Pierre had nearly run over Joe.

Jacques's SeaZoom hit the obstacle as though it were hitting a brick wall. The boat stopped suddenly, flipped in the air, and threw Jacques from the saddle. The villain somersaulted and crashed into the chilly water. The blow knocked Jacques unconscious, but his life vest brought him to the surface and kept his head above water.

"What goes around comes around," Joe said with a grin. "You know, I almost hate to call water rescue for these yahoos."

Frank chuckled. "Let's call it in and then get that guy who stole Curtis's boat," he said.

They made the radiophone call to the authorities as they sped down the lake, looking for some sign of the other craft.

"He's got a really big start on us," Joe called to his brother. "We'll be lucky to catch this guy."

"That's assuming he kept going," Frank said. "I'm betting that he'd abandon the SeaZooms and use some other, faster, form of transportation once he's gotten what he wants."

Joe frowned. "Then we'll still be lucky to catch him. Throttle up and keep your eyes peeled!"

They sped north for another five minutes, skirting the coast of Grand Isle, looking for any sign of the black racer. As they passed a large, forested island on the right, Joe pointed.

"There he is!"

The intruder's SeaZoom was pulled up on a strip of sand along the island's shore. Curtis's stolen watercraft bobbed in the water next to the other SeaZoom.

The brothers pulled into the shallows and hopped off their jetboats. They splashed over to the two crafts. The equipment hatch under the seat of Curtis's SeaZoom had been thrown open and its contents emptied.

"I think it's a safe bet that that guy found what he was looking for," Frank said.

"Let's just hope he hasn't gone too far with it," Joe replied. "Come on," he said, pointing to a line of tracks in the sand. "It looks like he went inland."

Experience had prepared the brothers to track a person through the woods in broad daylight, and the Hardys had no difficulty picking out the intruder's trail. Frank left his helmet behind so that it wouldn't hinder his vision, and he'd left his walkie-talkie behind because Joe had lost his when his SeaZoom sank. The brothers took their emergency radiophones, though, so they could summon the authorities if they found the bandit.

"How could he get off this island?" Joe asked as they pushed through the foliage. "Do you think he has another boat stashed somewhere?"

"Could be," Frank said. "Leaving the boat he used to commit the crime behind would be a smart idea. Or maybe someone's picking him up."

"Either way, let's hope we find the guy before he makes his connection," Joe said. He rounded a big pine tree and then stopped and motioned for Frank to do the same. "Hold on," he whispered.

"What?" Frank asked, coming to a halt.

"Listen."

Both brothers stood silently and listened for a few moments.

"I can hear someone talking," Frank said, "but I can't make out what he's saying."

"There's only one voice, though," Joe whispered. "If it's the same guy we trailed in Montreal, maybe he's on his cell phone again."

"If he is," Frank said, creeping forward cautiously, "he's going to find out that Pierre and Jacques have been disconnected."

Joe smiled and crept silently after his brother. They moved through the brush as quickly as they could while making almost no noise. The going was slower than either of them would have liked, but they hoped that moving silently would give them the element of surprise over their foe.

As they neared the other side of the island, the woods opened into a wide clearing. On the far side of the clearing, the Hardys saw water glistening beyond the woods. Standing at the opposite edge of the clearing was a man dressed in a black leather jacket and jeans. A large backpack dangled from his left shoulder. A black racing helmet covered his head and he had a cell phone pressed close to the side of the helmet. Just as Joe had surmised, the man was talking on the phone.

". . . went perfectly," the man said, his voice muffled by the helmet. "Yeah. I'm at the arranged spot now. I'll see you when you get here."

As the bandit spoke, Joe and Frank crept forward across the clearing. The brothers moved apart as they went, hoping to catch the criminal from both sides.

When they were within twenty feet of their quarry, the man hung up his cell phone.

Suddenly, he spun. He held a gun in his gloved right hand.

He pointed the weapon at the brothers.

"Take another step," he said, "and you're dead."

15 The Final Deception

The bandit chuckled. "You guys are quiet," he said, "but this helmet doesn't make me completely deaf. What does it take to get rid of you two, anyway?"

"More than you and your thugs have got," Joe said. "You'll never get away with this, you know." Try as he might, the younger Hardy couldn't make out the bandit's face beneath the dark-visored helmet. The faceplate muffled the man's voice as well, effectively disguising it.

This time the criminal actually laughed. "I've *already* gotten away with it," he said. "You two are a minor inconvenience, at best. Just a rest stop on the way to my big payday. What did you do with Pierre and Jacques, anyway?"

"Left them floating in the lake," Frank replied.

"Where the cops can pick them up," Joe added.

"Well," the man said, "I'm impressed—but not too impressed. Jacques and Pierre were expendable anyway."

"Just like Curtis, Collins, and Frid?" Joe asked.

The man in black nodded. "Yeah, just like those three."

"They didn't really have any idea what you're up to, did they?" Frank said.

"No more than you boys do," the man replied.

"You'd be surprised what we know," Joe said.

"For instance, it's hardly worth all this trouble to smuggle a few prescription meds from Canada into the U.S.," Frank said. "But experimental meds—ones based on secret formulas, that's a whole different story."

"We heard the reports about the pharmaceutical plant break-in and the stolen medicine on the news," Joe said. "They didn't seem to have anything to do with the race, so it took us a while to put two and two together."

"You guys are pretty smart after all," the man said. "But not smart enough to beat me at this late stage of the game. My ride will be here any minute, and you two are going to sit tight until it comes."

"A question before you go," Frank said. "How many of the race's accidents did you arrange?"

The man chuckled. "The ski lift, your bike and Victoria Clemenceau's, poor Georges's trouble—of course—and Baldwin's boat."

"Of course," Joe added, nodding slowly. "And the rest were merely normal accidents?"

"You've got it," the man said. "My employer figured that if the race officials had enough trouble to keep them busy, they wouldn't tumble to our smuggling plan. And now that I've answered your questions," he said, waving the gun at the brothers, "I want you to take off your emergency radios and throw them against that tree." He indicated a big pine at the edge of the clearing. "That way, I won't have you making any trouble for me and my ride."

"They'll catch you anyway, you know," Frank said.

"I doubt it," the man replied. "They don't have any more idea who I am than you do."

Frank and Joe exchanged a quick glance, but the man didn't notice.

"Now, get rid of those phones," the helmeted man said. "I'd rather not shoot you—but I will if I have to. You can leave this island sadder and wiser, or you can leave on stretchers. Your choice." He leveled the gun first at one Hardy and then at the other.

Frank and Joe unhooked the emergency phones from their belts. As they did so, Frank glanced at Joe and narrowed his eyes slightly. Joe nodded almost imperceptibly. Frank threw his phone at the tree, hard and fast. As it whizzed by the bandit, the man flinched slightly.

In that split second, Joe threw his phone directly into the criminal's faceplate. The visor shattered, momentarily blinding the man in black. The villain fired wildly, his shot hitting the ground to the left of Frank's feet.

Frank sprinted forward and kicked the gun out of the bandit's hand. His sight obscured by the broken visor, the villain staggered backward. Joe swung at his chin as the bandit backed away, but the man ducked his head just in time.

He ripped off his helmet and threw it at Joe. Joe dodged but not fast enough. The helmet caught him in the gut and knocked the wind out of him. He collapsed to his knees.

Frank pressed his attack with another kick and a karate chop, but the man blocked them both.

"Roger Baldwin!" Frank said.

Baldwin snarled at the brothers and dropped the backpack so he could move better. "You should have made it easy on yourselves," Baldwin said. "Now I'm gonna have to hurt you—permanently." He kicked for Frank's knee, but the older Hardy dodged out of the way.

"Big talk for a washed-up former triathlete," Joe said, rising to his feet once more.

"I've still got plenty to take care of you two," Baldwin replied. He threw a punch at Frank and then spun and kicked at Joe's head.

Joe blocked the kick and brought his elbow down hard on Baldwin's knee.

Baldwin grunted and spun away. Before he could recover, though, Frank came at him again.

The older Hardy threw three quick jabs at Baldwin's face and chest. The criminal easily blocked these, but he didn't see Frank's counterattack coming. As Baldwin warded off Frank's punches, Frank dropped into a spin kick and swept the bandit's legs out from under him.

Baldwin toppled over backward. He tried to get back up, but Joe jumped forward and punched him in the face as he rose. The bandit grunted and fell back, barely conscious.

"Not so tough without his friends, is he?" Joe said.

"Joe, duck!" Frank cried. He pushed his brother out of the way as a spray of bullets rained down from above.

Overhead, a two-person helicopter with the letters LMP stenciled on the tail hovered just above the trees. The pilot leaned out the side and sprayed a machine pistol toward the brothers.

"Looks like Baldwin's not out of friends yet," Frank said as he and Joe dived for cover.

The helicopter arced over the clearing, as if it might set down near Baldwin.

"Must be Baldwin's ride," Joe said, taking cover behind a big tree as the pilot shot at him.

Frank rolled to one side and scooped Baldwin's helmet off the ground. He heaved it with all his might toward the chopper's rear rotor. The helmet hit the small blades on the tail and ricocheted back into the main propeller.

Something popped and the chopper began to spin crazily, smoke spewing from near the rotors. The pilot dropped his gun and wrestled with the steering column. The helicopter lurched up into the air and disappeared over the trees.

Baldwin rose to his feet. "Come back!" he cried weakly. He staggered toward where his gun had fallen.

Joe rushed forward and punched Baldwin across the jaw. Baldwin collapsed in a heap, unconscious. Through the trees, the brothers saw the helicopter crash into the chilly waters of Lake Champlain.

Joe kneeled beside Baldwin and fished out the criminal's cell phone.

"Good thing Baldwin had this," Joe said, dialing 911, "or it might have been a while before he and his friend got medical attention."

Frank chuckled.

By nightfall the police had locked up the criminals and delivered the brothers to the finish line of the Speed Times Five Adventure Race. Chet and Jamal were relieved to see their friends, even though Frank and Joe had called their crew right after phoning the authorities.

Vince Bennett also seemed glad to see the Hardys.

"Great job, guys," he said. "Without you, the race might have turned into a disaster." The race organizer threw his burly arms across the Hardys' shoulders. "Now, if you'll just step this way, the media are waiting."

"Hold on a minute," Joe said.

"We told you earlier, we're not much for publicity," Frank added.

"Yeah," Joe said. "We're not the real story here. The press should be talking to the cops—

and whoever won the race. Um . . . who *did* win the race?"

"Kelly Hawk," Jamal said.

"You should have seen it," Chet said. "She and Lupin were neck and neck right up until the finish line."

"It was a great finish," Bennett agreed. "Best ever in one of my races."

"I guess this means she'll be getting all the publicity she needs for her cause," Frank said.

"Sure," Bennett said. "The media are on it already. UAN is talking about doing a special report about her tribe and their concerns."

"Great," Joe said. "We wouldn't want to take any attention away from that."

Bennett looked a bit crestfallen. "Are you sure? There's a great story here. It could be a feather in your caps if you want to be *real* detectives one day."

"No thanks," Frank said, chuckling. "I think we've had enough excitement for a while."

"Well, okay," Bennett said. "You're always welcome in any race I run, though. I'll even waive the fees."

"Thanks," the brothers said simultaneously.

"How did you figure the saboteur was Baldwin?" Jamal asked.

"The saboteur outraced us twice," Frank said. "Once in the woods near St. Esprit and again in Montreal. You have to be in good shape to do that."

"That meant that whoever was causing the trouble

was a trained athlete—probably one of the top competitors," Joe said.

"The thing about sabotage," Frank said, "is that you don't have to actually do it many times. After a couple of incidents, people start to get paranoid and see sabotage everywhere. Baldwin gummed up the chairlift mechanism, messed with Joe's brakes and Victoria's spokes, and clobbered Georges Clemenceau in the woods."

"He arranged his own accident as well," Joe added, "both to cover his tracks and so he could slip away for the payoff. But the other problems were purely bad luck. Landslides, bike problems, kayak accidents . . . all just coincidence—though Baldwin couldn't have done better if he'd planned them himself."

"Races always have *some* accidents," Bennett said.

"Baldwin might have made more mischief at St. Esprit, if we hadn't interrupted him," Frank concluded. "I'm sure he was constantly checking on Collins, Frid, and Curtis, as well as trying to see where they had the meds stashed."

"He'd need to know that to protect the goods during the race," Jamal added.

"I still can't believe that those three were in on this scheme," Chet said.

"They were and they weren't," Joe replied. "They knew they were smuggling *something*, but they didn't actually know what it was. They thought it was just some harmless prescriptions—not a stolen prototype medicine."

Frank nodded. "I wondered why Baldwin helped Maggie Collins on the river, then never stopped to help any other racers who got in trouble," he said. "When we discovered she was part of a smuggling ring, it all became clear."

"Baldwin didn't know whether she had the meds in her boat that day," Joe said. "He had to help her, because he couldn't take the chance that she'd go down with the loot."

"Baldwin stuck pretty close to the three of them all during the race," Frank said. "That was his job, to keep an eye on the 'couriers' and then to take the goods away from them when the time came. The only time Baldwin moved ahead of the students was on the last day—when he needed the extra time to set up his boating 'accident.'"

"After that he hooked up with Jacques and Pierre—who were planted as part of the medical crew by Baldwin's boss, Philippe LaTelle," Joe said.

"The pharmaceutical manufacturer who supplied the EMTs for the race?" Bennett asked.

"Yeah," Frank said. "We saw his limo near the hotel in Montreal. It was only much later that I realized the license plate I saw part of could have been LMP001—the kind of vanity plate suitable for the head of LaTelle Medical and Pharmaceutical. He'd arranged to have the meds stolen from a competitor, then set up the smuggling scheme. He was also the pilot of the helicopter that came to pick up Baldwin."

"If you want something done right, do it yourself," Jamal commented.

"With his skill and conditioning, Baldwin could have done a lot better in the race if he'd really been trying," Joe said.

"So he was never really interested in the race," Chet said.

"The money probably wasn't worth his time," Joe replied. "Smuggling stolen experimental pharmaceuticals probably paid much better."

"Or it would have," Jamal said, "if he'd gotten away with it."

"Which he didn't, thanks to you two," Bennett put in. "Why'd Baldwin and his boss try to cut those kids out, though?"

"Why take the chance that Collins, Curtis, and Frid might be discovered by customs officials at the end of the race?" Frank said.

"Plus, by stealing the goods from them, Baldwin and LaTelle wouldn't have to pay Curtis and the rest," Joe added. "Why pay for a botched smuggling assignment?"

"If you guys hadn't been there, it might have worked," Jamal said.

"If we hadn't heard the reports about the break-in and theft on the radio," Frank said, "we might never have tumbled to the real scheme."

"Good thing we paid attention to the news," Joe said. "Even if we didn't remember the news stories right away."

"Speaking of work," Bennett said. "I've got to get back to my job. And— Oh! I nearly forgot." He dug into one of the many pockets on his khaki vest and pulled out some papers. "I spoke to the race sponsors. They wanted to reward you all for what you've done. So, here are four weeklong passes to the Fire Creek Mountain Resort, all expenses paid. Use 'em at your leisure. You may not have won the race, but you did something just as important."

"Thanks," said Joe and Frank.

"Great!" Chet said, his eyes lighting up. "That means we've all got a free vacation whenever we want it!"

Joe and Frank rubbed their many bruises and glanced at each other. After six days of competition, they were beat.

"I don't know about the rest of you," Joe said, "but Frank and I could use that vacation right *now*."

2314

BILL WALLACE

Award-winning author Bill Wallace brings you fun-filled animal stories full of humor and exciting adventures.

Published by Simon & Schuster

648-32